The First Time Ever Published!

The 13th Donut Mystery

From *New York Times* Bestselling Author

Jessica Beck

DEEP FRIED HOMICIDE

Other Books by Jessica Beck

The Donut Shop Mysteries

Glazed Murder
Fatally Frosted
Sinister Sprinkles
Evil Éclairs
Tragic Toppings
Killer Crullers
Drop Dead Chocolate
Powdered Peril
Illegally Iced
Deadly Donuts
Assault and Batter
Sweet Suspects
Deep Fried Homicide

The Classic Diner Mysteries

A Chili Death
A Deadly Beef
A Killer Cake
A Baked Ham
A Bad Egg
A Real Pickle
A Burned Out Baker

The Ghost Cat Cozy Mysteries

Ghost Cat: Midnight Paws
Ghost Cat 2: Bid for Midnight

Jessica Beck is the *New York Times* Bestselling Author of the Donut Shop Mysteries,
The Classic Diner Mystery Series, and The Ghost Cat Cozy Mysteries.

To my spouse, for making it all possible in the first place!

Chapter 1

I was two rooms away getting a beer when I heard the apartment door break open.

Someone, most likely a cop, yelled, "Freeze," and the next thing I knew, two guns went off at the same time. I was Morton's partner in crime; we'd killed together, making us a weird kind of blood brothers, but I wasn't about to hang around to see who was alive, and who was dead. Where there was one cop, more would surely follow.

Revenge would have to wait until later.

At the moment, I just had to get out of there as fast as I could before a shot headed my way.

Chapter 2

My day began like most others at Donut Hearts. Honestly, after awhile, they tended to blur together. I woke up before anyone in her right mind would ever consider crawling out of bed, and I would soon begin making donuts with my assistant, Emma Blake, in the predawn hours of our sleepy little town of April Springs. Once that was accomplished, Emma and I would open the shop to let our customers in. After that, it was a matter of serving our small but loyal fan base until we finally locked our doors an hour before noon, unless it was one of those rare days where we sold out early. I tried to make sure that didn't happen, but it was a delicate dance between making enough donuts for the day without having to get rid of too many after we were closed. By the time my day at Donut Hearts was over, I was usually worn out and ready to go home, take a shower, and grab a quick nap. Today wasn't all that different, at least not so far, but I was due to have dinner with my best friend, Grace Gauge, later that night, and that made it special.

We never made it to the meal, though.

A possibility that I'd been dreading for years managed to kill that plan completely.

I just didn't know it yet.

When the dark stranger dressed in a severe suit came into my shop just before closing, I thought at first that it might be someone trying to get a last-minute donut before we locked our doors for the day.

How I wish that was all that it had been.

"Are you Suzanne Hart?" the man asked me in a stern voice.

"I am indeed," I said. "And if you're looking for donuts, I can make you a pretty sweet deal on what I have left."

"I'm afraid that's not what this is about," he said. There was a moment's hesitation, and then he added, "I'm here about Jake Bishop," as he took out a badge that looked all too familiar to me. I'd seen Jake's enough; that was for sure.

"Is he okay?" I asked as my hand reached for the counter to steady myself. It was the worst nightmare for *anyone* close to a law enforcement officer, whether the visit came at noon or midnight.

"I'm sorry, but there's been an incident," the man said.

"An incident? What happened?" I tried to breathe, but my lungs didn't seem to work. "Is he… dead?"

"No, but he's been wounded in the line of duty. I've been told that Officer Bishop is going to be okay, but he wanted you to know what happened before he'd let the doctors in the emergency room work on him."

"I need to be with him," I said as I grabbed my bag and my jacket. "Is he still in Hickory?"

"He is, but there's no rush. I've been told that no one will be able to see him for at least an hour."

"Where exactly was he shot?" I asked as I tried to wrap my head around the news.

"In an apartment just outside of Hickory's city limits," the officer explained.

"I don't care about the location!" I snapped. "Where on his body was he injured?"

The man nodded in understanding. "Officer Bishop took one round to the upper right arm just as he was returning fire. From what I understand, they were going to clean the wound and stitch him up as soon as I contacted you. According to what I was told, the bullet didn't do any major damage, so he should be back up on his feet in no time."

"How about the person who shot him?" I asked. Jake had been fairly close by lately, tracking down a madman who was killing circuit court judges. It was a high priority case, and he'd been working with all sorts of other law enforcement agencies trying to catch the madman.

"The suspect was killed instantly," the state policeman said.

Was it odd that I didn't shed a single tear for the man

who'd shot my boyfriend, the one true love of my life? His fate didn't even really matter to me at the moment. "Emma," I yelled to my assistant in back. "You're in charge, and I mean right now! I've got to go."

"What's going on?" my assistant asked as she came out from the kitchen, her hands still covered in sudsy soap. Emma might be young, but she was dependable, and I knew that I could trust her to run Donut Hearts in my absence.

"Somebody shot Jake. It looks as though he's going to be okay, but I'm going to Hickory to be with him."

A look of grave concern swept over her face. "Go, and don't worry about the shop."

"To be honest with you, I don't care if it burns to the ground right now." It surprised me that I meant it, too. The state policeman was standing between me and the donut shop's front door, something that happened to be a big mistake at the moment. "Either get out of the way or prepare to be run over," I said.

"I'm supposed to drive you," he said, clearly a little unsettled by my aggression.

"Then let's go," I said. "I need to be with Jake."

Chapter 3

As soon as we got into his unmarked squad car, I was glad that the state policeman was driving, because I was a nervous wreck, despite his assurance that Jake was going to be okay. As he started to drive, it began to lightly rain, and the sky darkened with intensity.

The weather matched my mood perfectly.

I suddenly realized that I didn't even know the man's name. "I know that I should have asked you earlier, but what's your name?"

"I'm Officer Hanlan," he said.

"Do you have a first name, Officer Hanlan?"

He smiled slightly for the first time since I'd met him. "It's Terry."

"Hi, Terry, it's nice to meet you," I said automatically. In all honesty, I wished that I'd never met him, at least not under the current circumstances.

"It's good to meet you, too," he said. "I'm truly sorry about Jake."

"Do you know him well?" I asked as I looked out the window as the clouds began to darken even more. It appeared that we were in for a storm.

He turned his wipers on as he said, "As a matter of fact, we went to the academy together. Miss Hart, try not to worry about him too much. Jake's one of the toughest officers I've ever known."

"I don't have any trouble believing that, but he's still lousy at stopping bullets."

That shut Terry up, though I didn't mean for it to do that. I thought about Grace just then. "I need to make a few telephone calls. Do you mind?"

"Go right ahead," he said.

I almost dialed Grace's number first, but I knew that there was someone else I had to talk to first.

"Hello," my mother said when she picked up.

"Momma, somebody just shot Jake," I said, the words coming out in a rush. Tears mixed in with my words. I tried to stop them, but I couldn't help it. I'd held it together so far, but just hearing my mother's voice was enough to send me spiraling out of control.

"Take a breath, Suzanne," Momma said calmly, "and tell me what happened."

"He was tracking down a killer in Hickory and he got shot," I said.

"How is he?" Momma asked in measured tones.

"He's in the emergency room at the moment, but they think he's going to be okay."

After a slight pause, Momma said with a sigh of relief, "That's wonderful news. Suzanne, stay right where you are, and I'll come and get you. We'll go together."

"I'm riding with a state policeman to Hickory even as we speak," I said, dabbing at my nose a little. At least I'd been able to rein in the tears.

"That's good. I'll meet you there. Which hospital is he in?"

"Hang on a second. I'll check." I covered the phone and asked Terry, "Where is he?"

"Catawba Memorial," he said.

"He's at Catawba," I said, relaying the information to Momma.

"I'll see you there, then," she said.

"Thanks, Momma," I answered barely above a whisper.

"It's going to be all right. I love you, sweetie."

"I love you, too," I said. I suddenly realized that I couldn't stand another conversation, not even with my best friend. "Would you call Grace and explain what happened?"

"Don't you worry about a thing. I'll see you soon."

"Thank you," I said, and then I hung up.

The tears suddenly came again as I ended the call, flowing so hard I could barely see.

Terry reached out a hand and patted my shoulder. In a

soothing voice, he said, "He's going to be okay, Suzanne."

"I'll believe it when I see it," I said. I managed to corral my crying jag again, knowing that when I did finally get to see Jake, I didn't want him to see me sobbing hysterically.

The short drive to Hickory seemed to take a lifetime. When we finally got there, a uniformed local police officer met us at the emergency room after we made our way through a crowd of reporters mingling near the entrance. "Officer Hanlan?" he asked my escort.

"That is correct," Terry said.

"The doctor's right over there," he said. "She's been waiting for you."

"Good," Terry replied as he led me to a youthful woman wearing scrubs. Wow, she was young. The doctor couldn't have been out of her twenties, and her blonde hair pulled back into a ponytail didn't help matters. This was the woman who had Jake's life in her hands?

"Are you Suzanne Hart?" she asked me as soon as we approached her.

"I am. How is he, Doctor?"

"No worries. Officer Bishop is going to be just fine," the young doctor said.

"Are you sure?" I asked, not daring to let myself believe her. I suddenly realized how I must be coming across. "I didn't mean that the way that it sounded."

"I understand completely," she said with a smile. "For a gunshot wound, it wasn't too bad, but he's going to need some time to recover. He'll need to stay here overnight, and then we'll release him. After that, he's going to need about a month to get the full use of his arm back. During that time, he's going to have to wear his arm in a sling."

I'd forgotten that Terry was standing behind me. In a low voice, he said, "Jake's going to just *love* that."

"I'll make sure that he does everything that he needs to do," I said, and then I turned back to the doctor. "When can I see him?"

"I'll take you to him right now," she said as she put the tablet in her hands down onto the counter. "Be warned, though, he's going to be a little woozy. We gave him something for the pain. I've got to say that the man really must love you, Miss Hart. He made me promise that I'd take care of you personally before he'd even let me touch his wound."

"That's good to hear, but he can't love me nearly as much as I love him," I said.

The doctor smiled at me, but it faded quickly as she noticed the throng of reporters moving toward us. "Get them out of here," she told the officer on duty.

Terry responded as well. "I'll give him a hand."

"Why are there so many reporters and cameras here?" I asked. "Are you taking care of someone famous?"

"Didn't you know? They're all here for your boyfriend," the doctor said, clearly surprised by my question. "After all, he's a hero."

"He's always been special in my eyes, but honestly, I don't care what they think he is. I'm just glad that he's going to be okay."

"Let's just ignore them then, shall we? Would you like to come with me?"

That's when I heard a commotion behind me near where the reporters were being herded away.

My mother's voice rang through the crowd loudly. "My daughter is standing right there, so you're going to have to shoot me to stop me from joining her."

"It's okay," I told Terry, and he let her through.

Momma hugged me, and then I told her the good news. "Jake is going to be okay. I hate to just ditch you like this, but I get to go see him right now."

"Then go," Momma said with a smile. "I'll be right here when you get back. And Suzanne?"

"Yes, Momma?"

"Give him my best," she said.

"Right after I'm done giving him mine," I said with the

first smile I'd had in what felt like months.

"Hey, there," Jake said groggily as he opened his eyes. He smiled slightly, and then he winced a little.

"Are you okay?" I asked him.

"Do you mean other than the fact that I'm feeling like I've been shot, drugged, and stitched up with a huge needle and thread? Honestly, I'm fine," Jake said, doing his best to manage a grin.

"I'm so glad that you're okay," I said as I started to hug him. He was hooked up to some monitors, which started beeping immediately.

A nurse came over to check on him. "Is everything all right here?"

"Trust me. If my heart doesn't start pumping harder whenever I see her, you'd better get new machines, or pull the plug altogether," Jake told her with a slight smile.

She smiled in return as she patted his arm gently. "Just take it easy, okay?"

"Yes, ma'am," he said. "I promise."

Jake tried to rub his eyes, but he couldn't quite manage it. "Suzanne, can I have a sip of water?"

"Let me check," I said, and I hurried to the nurse's station. "He wants some water."

"Certainly," she said as she filled a cup halfway and then handed it to me.

"That will do," I replied as I took it from her and then ferried it to him.

After a few sips, Jake sighed. "Boy, is happiness ever relative. If you'd have told me yesterday that I'd be satisfied with that, I would have called you crazy."

"I'm so happy that you're alive," I said as I stroked his forehead lightly. "I couldn't stand the thought of losing you. I love you. You know that, don't you?"

He smiled gently back at me, and I was glad that I wasn't the one wearing the heart monitor. "With all my heart. I love you, too, and you were never in danger of losing me."

I looked at him incredulously. "You do remember that you were just shot, don't you?"

"I remember," he said as he winced a little. "He got off a lucky shot at the same time I pulled the trigger myself, that's all." After a moment, Jake asked, "Do you know what happened to him?"

"You got him," I said. Surely he had to have remembered that. Most likely he was foggy from the meds he was on. "It's okay, Jake."

"I didn't have any choice," he said softly, and then he frowned as his monitor started getting louder.

"I'm sorry, but I'm afraid that you'll have to go now," the same nurse who'd given me water for Jake said.

"Is he okay?"

"He's fine," she reassured me. "He just needs some rest."

"I'll see you soon," I said as I patted his leg on the way out.

"You can count on it," he replied.

Momma was in the waiting room when I got back out there, but she wasn't alone. The reporters were all gone, but I was thrilled to see that Grace was sitting with her. They both hugged me and started talking at the same time.

"Take it easy, you two," I said, happy to be with them both. "Jake's doing fine."

"I cannot *believe* that someone shot him," Grace said. "The worst thing that happens to me in my job is that I get scolded every now and then."

"I confess," Momma added, "that the perils of what I do are equally mundane." She turned back to me and asked, "How did he look?"

"Like a million bucks," I said, an expression my dad used to say when he'd still been with us.

Momma nodded. "Here, I got you some coffee," she said as she handed me a cup. "I'm afraid that it's not piping hot, and even if it were, it would still be borderline at best. It's nowhere near as good as the coffee you and Emma serve at Donut Hearts."

"I'm just grateful for anything at the moment," I said as I took a sip. She was right on all counts, but I didn't mind. I had Jake back after nearly losing him forever, and that was really all that mattered to me.

"When does he get out of here?" Grace asked as she looked around the waiting room. "There was a crowd of reporters outside when I drove up, and the only reason that *I* got through was that your mother was there to vouch for me." She turned to Momma and said with a smile, "I bet you regret that already."

"Never," Momma said as she patted my best friend's hand.

"Thanks for coming, you two," I said, "but Grace, shouldn't you be working right now? I thought you had a big day scheduled."

"I did, but I can always shift things around for you," she said.

"I'm fine, and Jake is, too. Thanks for coming, but you need to go back to work. I'll call you if there's any change, or if I need anything. I promise."

"Are you sure? I don't want to just abandon you here," Grace said with a little reticence in her voice. I knew she was swamped with work, but she would beg off doing any of it if I let her.

"Don't worry, dear. She always has me," Momma said.

"That she does," Grace said, and then she stood. "If you're absolutely sure, then there a few things that I really need to do."

"Go," I said as I stood and hugged her. "I'll talk to you later."

"Give him a kiss for me when you see him," Grace said as she was leaving.

"I will, but it's going to have to wait until all of mine are delivered first," I said with a grin.

Once Grace was gone, I told Momma, "The same goes for you, you know. I understand that you have a busy life yourself."

"There's nothing I'd rather be doing, and no one I'd rather be with right now than you," she said.

"Thanks, for everything," I replied.

"It's my pleasure. Now stop thanking me."

"Yes, ma'am," I replied with a grin.

After a few moments, Momma said, "You know, once Jake is out of here, he's going to need somewhere to go to recuperate. Have you given that any thought?"

"To be honest with you, I'm still wrapping my head around the idea that he got shot this morning."

"I understand that, but I want to make you an offer that I'm serious about you taking. Before you say no out of hand, I want you to seriously consider it. Is that agreed?"

"Sure," I said, wondering what she had in mind. "What's going on?"

"Suzanne, I know that you're not aware of this, but I recently bought a house on the other edge of town as an investment. I propose that I move out of our cottage immediately and stay there."

I started to protest, but she held up a hand and silenced me, something that no one else had ever managed to do. "Let me finish. You promised, remember?"

"Okay," I said. "Go on."

"Jake can take over my bedroom downstairs. After all, he's in no shape to climb stairs. We both know that you can take better care of him at the cottage than you can anywhere else, and I want him to take as long as he needs to get better. You know, the more I think about it, the better I like it. It's actually quite perfect. The park is right there, so when he's up to it, he can even walk for exercise. What do you say?"

I started to say no automatically, but the more I thought about it, the more I realized just how ideal a solution it would be. After a few moments, I said, "I'll have to run it by him, but it sounds perfect to me, if you're sure that you don't mind. It's only going to be a month."

She grinned at me and hugged me tightly. "It can take as long as it takes, Suzanne. There's no timeframe on my offer.

Thank you for letting me do this for you."

"Like I said, we'll both have to persuade him that it's a good idea first."

Momma grinned. "Don't worry about that. You just leave it all to me."

Chapter 4

It took some convincing, but by the time Jake was ready to be discharged from the hospital, he'd agreed to our plan.

I hadn't been standing idly by waiting for him to be discharged, though. There was a great deal of work to do, including moving Momma to her new, if temporary, digs.

"How on earth did I ever manage to accumulate so many worthless things?" Momma asked me as we loaded another box into the sheriff's pickup truck. Actually, it didn't belong to Chief Martin; it was his cousin's, but he'd graciously allowed us to use it for the move.

"What are you talking about, Dorothea? This isn't junk," the police chief said as he hoisted a box. "These are all full of precious memories."

"I don't know about that," Momma said, but she smiled at him as she said it. The two of them had grown incredibly close over the last few months, and I couldn't help wondering if we'd have an actual wedding soon. There had been a false alarm with Emily Hargraves and Max, my ex-husband, but I doubted that Momma and the sheriff would change their minds if they ever decided to get married in the first place.

"I still don't know why you're moving so many of your things in the first place," I told Momma as I surveyed the boxes and boxes of her personal possessions still stacked on the front porch of the cottage we shared. "You're only going to be gone for a month, and then we're going to have to just move everything back in again."

"About that," Momma said gravely. "We need to talk, Suzanne."

"I'll see about finishing loading that truck," the police chief said as he grabbed another box from the porch.

"You do that, Phillip," Momma said. "Suzanne, let's go inside and have a cup of tea and chat."

"Why don't I like the sound of this?" I asked my mother as

we walked back into the cottage together.

"It could be because you tend to worry too much," she said with a grin.

"Where on earth could I have gotten that?" I asked her. My mother was a champion worrier when it came to our family, and she'd passed the trait down to me long ago.

"It must have been from your father's side," she said with a hazy bit of a smile. "Speaking of your father, he's been gone for quite a few years now."

"I know," I said. My dad might have been gone, but I could still hear his laugh in the cottage if I closed my eyes, though how much of that was due to my imagination I couldn't say.

"Suzanne, he would have wanted me to be happy," she said as she squeezed my hands. "You know that, don't you?"

I was just too close to it. I had no idea where my mother was going with this conversation. "Of course he would have."

Momma took a deep breath, and then, in a rush of words she said, "I'm honoring his wishes. It's why I've accepted Phillip's proposal of marriage."

"You're getting married again?" I asked, incredulous that I hadn't seen this coming. Neither one of them were getting any younger, and it was clear, even to me, that they belonged together. "What I meant to say was congratulations," I added lamely with my best smile.

"Thank you," Momma replied, clearly relieved that I'd added my well wishes, if belatedly. "Suzanne, how do you feel about it, really? You can be honest with me. I know that you and Phillip have had your differences in the past."

"Sure, we've butted heads on occasion," I admitted, "and we probably will in the future, but that doesn't mean that I can't see that he's good for you. You've been happier over the past few months than you've been in a lot of years, Momma." I hugged her, squeezing my mother tight. "I'm really happy for you, and I mean it with all my heart." When I pulled away from her, I could see that she was crying.

"Momma, are you okay?"

"I'm fine, now," Momma said. "I was so afraid that you wouldn't approve."

I took my mother's hands in mine as I said, "Momma, even if I didn't, which I do, that still wouldn't mean that you shouldn't do what was best for you."

"My darling daughter, if you had a problem with this marriage, I would tell Phillip that I had a change of heart and I would retract my acceptance."

"You'd really do that for me?" I asked, having a hard time believing it.

"You are my only child, but there's more to it than that. Since you've come back here to live with me, you've become my best friend as well," Momma said. She wasn't usually so prone to sentiment, and it really touched me hearing her voice those feelings. Sure, she told me that she loved me often enough, but being called her best friend really touched me.

"You're my best friend, too," I said.

"Even over Grace?" she asked.

"It's only fair. After all, I've known you longer," I said with a laugh.

"Not by much," Momma answered with a hint of laughter of her own.

"So, does this mean that you're not coming back to live here, even after Jake recovers?" I asked as I looked around the cottage that we shared.

"Of course I'll be back," she said. "I just won't live here anymore."

A thought suddenly occurred to me. "Chief Martin isn't behind this move, is he?"

Momma looked surprised by the question. "Of course not. Why would you even ask such a thing?"

"Well, I wouldn't really blame him if he felt that way. After all, you and Dad lived here your entire married life. It would be hard for another man to try to live here, too."

"You should know that Phillip has never tried to replace

your father, not in your eyes, and certainly not in mine. He understands that the memories I have of your dad are more precious to me than anything in my life but you. No, Phillip would live wherever I chose, as long as he could join me. I need to do this for me. It's time for a fresh start."

"Does that mean that you're going to live together before the wedding?" I wasn't sure how I thought about that prospect, just because it was my own mother. It came as quite a shock to me to realize just how old fashioned I was.

"No, I'll move into the house now, and he'll join me after the ceremony. Believe it or not, I invited him to move in with me today, but he insisted that we follow convention and wed first."

"So, when are these nuptials going to take place?" I asked her.

"Well, neither one of us are getting any younger," she told me with a smile. "We thought the sooner the better. How does four weeks sound to you?"

"That's perfect," I said. "Jake should be fully recovered by then."

"Why do you think we chose that timeframe?" Momma asked me, grinning. "We want him there in good form when we say our vows."

"Thanks for that. Are you having a big blowout of a wedding?" I asked her.

"No, we've decided that we want only two witnesses with us."

"Jake and I are going to be your only guests?" I asked.

"If you'll be my maid of honor, Phillip is going to ask Jake to be his best man. What do you think he'll say?"

"I'm sure that he'll agree," I said. "I have one last question. Is this supposed to be a big secret, or can I tell anyone I want to?"

"You can broadcast it on the news for all I care," Momma said happily. Honestly, she was downright giddy about the prospects. "I have a feeling that Phillip might beat you to it, though. He's going to be absolutely jubilant when I tell him that you approve."

"May I tell him myself?" I asked. There had indeed been some ill feelings between us in the past, though those had mostly faded away. As a matter of fact, we'd even started cooperating lately on cases that I was involved in, something that still managed to surprise me. But there was still the hint of an undercurrent that I wanted to dispel once and for all.

"Of course," Momma said. "I'll go get him."

"Let me," I said.

She nodded. "Okay, but keep the door open. I want to hear his reaction."

I smiled at her. "You know that I'm going to have a little fun with him first, don't you?"

Momma smiled. "Of course I know it. Just don't give him too hard a time."

"We'll see how it goes," I said.

I opened the porch door to see the police chief standing close by gripping a box that held bath towels, a light enough load that he could hold it forever if he had to.

"Hey," I said in as neutral a voice as I could manage.

"Hi there," he replied, trying to act nonchalant, though I knew that the suspense had to be killing him.

"So listen," I said, adding a touch of iron to my voice, "I've just finished talking to my mother about your proposal."

"Let me explain," he said before I could tell him that I approved. "Suzanne, it should come as a surprise to no one that I'm in love with your mother. I admit that I'm shocked she feels the same way about me, but what she told you is the straight up truth. If you have a real problem with this, we'll call the whole thing off." Before I could break in, he added, "Not that I'm going to stop seeing her, no matter what your decision might be. It took me most of my life to convince her that we belong together, and I'm not about to throw that all away now."

"Nobody doubts that you love her, Chief," I said. "I just have one question for you."

"Go ahead and ask it, then," the chief said in a steady

voice.

"Are you going to do your best to make her happy for the rest of her life?"

He nodded. "With every breath I have left in me."

"Then I approve," I said, and to both our surprises, I hugged him. "Welcome to the family."

Momma came out just then, and as Chief Martin pulled away, I could swear that he was crying, ever so slightly. Taking out a bandana handkerchief, he dabbed at his eyes as he said, "The pollen count must be sky high today."

"I'm sure that it is," I said, and then I noticed that Momma was crying, too.

When did I start crying, though?

For such a happy occasion, there were certainly an awful lot of tears going around.

After unpacking all of Momma's things at her new place, a house that I'd admired for years for its Craftsman style architecture, I said my good-byes and left the newly engaged couple to their own devices. Momma had taken a great many of her personal items with her, but fortunately, she'd left most of her furniture behind at the cottage. The new place was already outfitted with everything that she needed, so I didn't have to go shopping for anything more than groceries anytime soon.

Driving my Jeep across town, I thought about ducking back into the donut shop and taking care of some inventory issues that I'd been putting off for weeks, but then I decided not to do it at the moment. After all, it was clearly just an excuse not to go back home now that I was alone and on my own. I hadn't lived by myself ever in my life, going from Momma's to the place that I'd shared with Max, and then back to Momma's again. In all of that time, I was willing to bet that I hadn't spent a handful of nights on my own, all by myself.

Jake wasn't due to arrive until the next day, and things would be crazy enough then, but for now, I was alone. I probably should have savored the moment, but when I walked back into the cottage that I had so recently shared with Momma, all I could feel was sad. Her absence was conspicuous, and not just because of all of the things that she'd taken with her. More important than her things was her presence, the spirit that had always made this a home and not a house.

I plopped down on the couch, wondering what I was going to do with myself, when there was a knock at my door.

Who could be visiting me now?

I was delighted to find Grace there when I opened it, a bottle of wine in her hand. "Hey, I saw you come back home. Since we had to cancel our plans tonight, would you care to share this with me?"

"Your timing couldn't be better," I said. "Boy, do I have news for you."

Grace looked delighted by the prospect. "Grab two glasses, and we can get started," she said.

I was happy that my best friend had sensed that I'd need her and she'd acted upon it. I wasn't going to be all alone tonight after all.

Chapter 5

"She's getting married?" Grace asked with delight when I told her the news about Momma and the chief. "What do you think about it?"

"Honestly, I'm happy for them," I said, pleased that I could say it without stretching the truth in the least. "It's hard finding someone you want to spend the rest of your life with."

"Tell me about it," Grace said.

"Don't give me that. You've finally got a decent boyfriend of your own, which has to be a nice change of pace for you." Grace had recently started dating a police officer on the local force who happened to be a friend and customer of mine named Stephen Grant. Officer Grant had always been of help to me, even when his boss hadn't been nearly as supportive, and he was clearly smitten with Grace. I knew from watching her look at him that she was just as intrigued as he was.

"He's really quite nice, even if he is kind of young for me," Grace admitted, "but we're a long way from doing anything as drastic as getting married."

"Do you think Momma's rushing things with the police chief?" I asked with a frown.

"No, of course not," Grace said quickly. "After all, they've known each other forever. This has been brewing for years. Nobody's rushing into anything!"

"I agree," I said.

"So, when's Jake getting here?" Grace asked me.

"I'm picking him up from the hospital tomorrow," I replied.

"Do you need a hand?"

I had to laugh. "I appreciate the offer, but I believe I can handle him."

"That's what you think now," Grace said, "but let me remind you that living together is something very different from dating."

"It's not like that, Grace," I said. "I'm going to be upstairs, and Jake is going to be in the master bedroom downstairs. He's here to recover, and that's all. There's not going to be any hanky-panky."

"Not even a little?" Grace asked me, clearly looking a little disappointed.

I laughed at her again. "From what the doctor told me, he's going to need all of his energy just recovering from his gunshot wound," I said. As I looked around the living room, I knew that Grace was right about one thing. It would be odd having someone besides Momma here with me, no matter how short the duration. I hoped that we didn't kill each other with kindness, tiptoeing around the place. Then again, I couldn't imagine Jake tiptoeing anywhere.

We'd be fine.

A little voice in my head added, "Keep telling yourself that and maybe it will come true."

I chose to ignore it.

After all, tomorrow would be there soon enough, and I still had a ton of work to do.

Grace and I ordered a pizza, and while we waited for it to be delivered, she helped me clean. By the time the food came, we were both ready for a break.

Sitting on the sofa eating, Grace asked me, "Suzanne, how is this new arrangement going to work with the donut shop?"

"I'm taking two weeks off, and then we're going to see how it goes from there," I said, trying to be as nonchalant as I could.

Grace stopped the slice of pizza headed for her mouth. "You're not shutting the place down for two solid weeks. I don't believe it."

"Don't worry, I'm not about to do that. Emma and her mother are going to run Donut Hearts for me while I stay here and take care of Jake."

"You won't last two days," Grace said flippantly.

"Hey, that donut shop isn't my entire life," I protested.

"Can you honestly tell me that you really believe that?"

"Okay, I'll admit that it's going to be tough," I said, "but Jake needs me. There are only three people in the world that I would do this for: Jake, Momma, and you."

"I'm touched," Grace said. "What does Jake think about your plans of being with him around the clock?"

"I haven't told him yet," I said as I bit my lip. "It's going to put us together during our entire waking moments, and to be honest with you, even though we've been dating for quite awhile, this could be a real stumbling block in our relationship."

"You could always look at it another way," she suggested.

"How's that?"

"Think of it as a perfect way to find out if you're right for each other in the end. If you can survive his recovery together, you can endure anything."

"I suppose you're right," I said. "But Grace, what if he gets tired of me and decides to break up with me after this is over?" I'd been fretting about that very thing since the plan for him to recover at the cottage had first been discussed. Saying it out loud just made the prospect of losing Jake even worse.

"That's impossible," Grace said as she put her pizza down and hugged me. "If you want my opinion, he's just going to end up loving you even more than he does right now."

"I hope you're right," I said with a heavy sigh as I picked up another piece of pizza. "Anyway, we'll find out soon enough."

"Just be sure to cut him a little slack," Grace said. "After all, he did just get shot."

"Not only that, but he barely fought his boss on the mandatory leave of absence they gave him. Jake told him that he wanted to stay out a week, but his boss insisted on the full month. The funny thing about it is that Jake didn't really put up that much of a fight. A part of me wonders if he even wants to go back to his old job."

"I can see how getting shot might do that to him."

"That's the thing, though. You don't know Jake," I explained. "He's *always* lived for his work. When his family was killed in that car accident, he told me that the job was the only thing that saved him. I'm not so sure he feels that way anymore."

"I totally get that. After all, he's got something else to live for now," Grace said.

"What's that?"

"You," she said.

"I don't want to lose him, that's for sure."

"You won't," Grace said.

After we finished the pizza, she looked around the cottage's living room. "This place looks pretty good. What else do we need to do? How's the master bedroom situation?"

"Momma already took care of that, and the kitchen, too. That just leaves the upstairs, and I'm not going to worry about that. It's going to be days before Jake has the strength or the energy to climb those steps."

"And the bathroom down here?" Grace asked. "Is there room for his stuff in there?"

"With Momma's things gone, he's got the entire run of the master suite."

Grace looked around once more, and then she added, "I can't believe that she's actually gone. Your mother has lived here as long as I've been alive."

"Me, too, but she told me that even if Jake hadn't been shot, she was going to move out anyway, so I don't feel so bad about evicting her. There were just too many memories here for her to start a new life with someone else. Too many ghosts around every corner, I guess."

"I can see that," Grace said. "Anyway, now that our work here is finished, would you like me to stay over with you? Take it from me, it can be awfully lonely being all by yourself in a big old house."

"You do it all of the time," I protested.

"Yeah, but I've always been tougher than you," she said with a laugh.

"We both know that's not true," I said. "Thanks for the offer, but I think I'm going to go solo tonight. Since it's going to be my only chance to do it for awhile, I want to embrace the experience."

"I understand, but if you get scared or lonely in the middle of the night, I'm just down the street, okay? I won't tease you if you decide to call me and ask me to come over here later." She paused, and then she added with a wicked grin, "Well, not much, anyway."

"I'll see you tomorrow, Grace," I said as I walked her out onto the porch. "This was fun. Exactly what I needed."

"You're most welcome. I had a good time, too."

Once she was gone, the cottage seemed to get awfully quiet. It wasn't that Momma was normally that loud, but I missed her presence there nonetheless. Looking around for something to do, I saw the pizza box still sitting on the coffee table, so I decided to throw it away outside so the living room wouldn't smell like pizza when Jake came tomorrow.

When I opened the front door, though, there was movement outside in the bushes.

"Grace, that's not funny," I said loudly.

There was no response.

I got out my cell phone and dialed Grace's number on speed-dial.

When she answered, my best friend said, "Wow! That was even faster than I thought it would be. I just walked through my own front door."

"Do you mean that you're not still here?" I asked as I peered out into the gloom. "Seriously?"

"Suzanne, like I said, I'm home. Wow, you really *are* jumpy, aren't you? No sweat, though. I'm on my way."

"No. Stay there. Please."

"Are you sure?" she asked, the uncertainty clear in her voice.

"Positive. I'm okay. Listen, I'm probably just jumping at

shadows. Once I'm back inside, I'm going to deadbolt the front door and light a fire." I glanced at my watch, and then I added, "On second thought, maybe I'll just call it a night and go to bed. I'm giving Emma and her mother a final run-through tomorrow at the donut shop, so I have to be up in five hours."

"Fine, but you have to promise that you'll call me if you need me, or if you see or hear anything else outside, okay? I mean it."

"I promise," I said as I walked back in and deadbolted the door. Just that action alone gave me a great deal of comfort. "But I have one question for you."

"What's that?"

"What are the two of us going to be able to do that I can't do on my own?"

"We can double-team the bad guy together," she said. "Isn't that enough?"

I paused and listened outside for a moment before I spoke again. "Now that I think about it, I'm sure that it was just the wind."

"I don't know. I'm looking out my window, and the trees seem kind of still over here," Grace said a little tentatively.

"Maybe the park has more of a breeze than you do."

"Sure, that's exactly what it is," she said. "I'll see you tomorrow, Suzanne. Sleep tight."

"You, too."

After we hung up, I walked all around the first floor of the cottage, turning the lights on and off as I inspected each room to make sure everything was locked up tight. I would have felt ridiculous doing it if anyone else had been there, but then again, if they had, I wouldn't have felt the compulsion to do it in the first place.

Tomorrow would be there soon enough, and I had a big day ahead of me, what with turning over the keys to the donut shop, then driving to Hickory and picking Jake up from the hospital. Getting him settled in would take some time, but after that, we were wide open.

It would be the beginning of our time living in the house together, even if it was only temporary.

I didn't want to think about that now, though.

There would be time enough to worry about all of that tomorrow.

For now, I really had to get some sleep.

"I can't thank you enough for doing this, Mrs. Blake," I told Emma's mother the next morning bright and early at Donut Hearts. "It's unbelievably kind of you to step in on such short notice."

"Nonsense," Emma's mother said. "It will absolutely be my pleasure working here with Emma every day. And don't you think it's time that we were on a first-name basis?"

"I suppose," I said, not sure how I felt about that. She'd been Mrs. Blake to me for as long as I'd known her.

"Call me Sharon," she said.

"I'll try, Sharon," I replied, but it felt weird calling her by her first name.

Emma asked, "Should I call you Sharon, too, Mom?"

"You'd better not, young lady," her mother told her with a smile. "There's only one person in the world who can rightfully call me mother, and I'm not missing out on that for anything. Is that okay with you?"

Emma hugged her mom as she said, "That's fine with me. I was just teasing." She turned to me and asked, "What should we do first, boss?"

"I'm just here today as an observer and an advisor in case anything goes wrong. This is your donut shop for the next two weeks. I'll try to sit back and not comment unless I see something dangerous about to happen."

"I'll believe that when I see it," Emma said, and then she turned to her mother. "Okay, Mom, are you ready to get started?"

"I can't wait," she said, and the two of them got to work. Sharon flipped on one of our coffee pots while Emma turned on the fryer, and the two of them worked in perfect tandem as they prepped for the first treats of the day, our cake donuts. I didn't know why I was all that surprised that they worked so well together. After all, the mother-daughter duo had filled in for me before, just not on such a long-term basis. While I was clearly the boss when Emma and I were there working alone, these two were equal partners. It was a pleasure to watch them, at least it was after I'd clamped down on myself from adding anything that wasn't completely necessary. They might not have done things my way, but their methods were certainly sound ones.

"How are we doing so far?" Emma asked after the cake donuts were finished and the dough was raising for the yeast ones. It was time for our traditional break, and the three of us were outside in the cool morning air.

"I'm taking notes on how to improve my techniques," I said, only partially joking.

"I'm sure that you're just being gracious," Sharon said.

"Honestly, the more I think about it, I'm not even sure why I'm here. You two clearly don't need me." It felt odd saying that about my own shop, and it was even stranger knowing that it was indeed true.

"Don't kid yourself, Suzanne. My daughter and I might be able to fill in while you're away," Sharon said, "but we'll never replace you, nor do either one of us ever want that. Do we, Emma?"

My assistant shook her head. "No way. I'm perfectly content with my usual role at Donut Hearts. This is going to be a tough few weeks, and I have a hunch that I'll be ready to get things back to normal as soon as we can. Not that I'm complaining or anything. Suzanne, you're doing the right thing taking care of Jake. He needs you more than this old donut shop does right now."

"I can see that," I said.

"How does he like all of the attention he's been getting in the press?" Sharon asked.

"He hates it," I said. "Jake was never one to go for the spotlight, and he can't wait until he's yesterday's news.

That's a direct quote, by the way."

"It will happen soon enough," Sharon said. "Tell him I said that he should enjoy it while he can."

"I would if I thought that it would do any good, but the man's just not built that way." The timer went off, and as the mother and daughter team headed back inside, I paused. "You two clearly have things under control here. If you don't mind, I think that I'm going to head back home and catch a quick nap before I have to pick Jake up."

"Are you sure?" Sharon asked. "We don't want to run you off from your own shop."

"I'm positive. Keep up the good work."

"You know that you can count on us. We won't let you down," Emma said, and then she hugged me.

"What was that for?"

"I think it's wonderful what you're doing for your boyfriend."

"He'd do the same thing for me if the roles were reversed," I said.

"Then you've found yourself a winner," Sharon said. She hesitated a moment, and then she asked, "We'll try not to bother you with any of the more mundane details around here, but is it okay if we call you now and then if we need you?"

"Are you kidding? I'm counting on it," I said. "To be honest with you, I'm not sure how I'm going to be able to stand being away from the shop, so a call every now and then would be greatly appreciated."

"We'll try not to disappoint you," Sharon said.

"You couldn't if you tried."

If felt odd leaving Donut Hearts in the darkness. On a normal day, I would have hours more work to do before we unlocked the front doors, and then it would be more time spent selling coffee and donuts until we closed for the day.

But today was anything but a normal day.

I drove home in the darkness, and to my shock, as I pulled

into the drive, I saw that the front door of the cottage was standing wide open.

The problem was that I knew that *I'd* locked it when I'd left.

Someone had obviously gone inside without my permission.

Chapter 6

I briefly thought about going in and checking out the cottage myself, but I'd been a part of too many investigations in the past to take a stupid chance like that. I hated it when people did crazy things on their own in movies or in books, so I wasn't about to echo their behavior in real life.

I slowly backed out of the drive and started to dial 911 when I saw a dark form rush out of the house into the darkness of the park just beyond our doorstep. I could probably go in now, but what if there was someone else still inside?

I finished dialing the emergency number, and I was surprised to get Chief Martin on the line.

"What are you doing at work at this time of morning?" I asked him.

"Ruthie stepped out for a minute, so I said I'd take over. Two of my people have the flu, so I'm pulling double shifts all week. What's going on, Suzanne?"

"Somebody just broke into the cottage."

"Are they still there?" he asked.

"Well, I just saw one person run out of my house and into the park," I said, "but that doesn't mean that somebody else isn't still inside."

"You're not thinking about going in and checking it out yourself, are you?"

"No way. I saw the door standing wide open when I pulled up. Whoever was inside must have seen me arrive, because when I started dialing 911, they ran away."

"Do not, I repeat, do not go into that house!" he said in a voice that would not tolerate disobedience.

"You don't have to worry about me," I said. "Just hurry."

"Don't do anything stupid. I'm on my way."

I decided that I'd probably be okay parked in the road where I was. If someone else came out of the house, or if the mysterious guest in the park decided to come after me, I'd be able to back down the street in reverse at least until I could turn around. Until the police chief got there, I spent every second scanning the immediate vicinity, searching for any sign that I might be in trouble, but I didn't see anything.

Chief Martin pulled up in his squad car, his lights on, but the siren silent. He quickly got out and walked over to me, so I opened the Jeep door.

"Have you seen anything else since we spoke?"

"I haven't seen a thing," I said.

"Wait right here," he ordered.

"Shouldn't you have backup?" I asked, worried what might happen to the police chief if he went in alone and someone bad was still inside. I'd never be able to face my mother again if anything I did caused her fiancé harm.

"Like I said before, we're short-handed, but Officer Grant is on his way. In the meantime, I'm going to have a look around."

The chief pulled out a large flashlight and held it next to his service revolver, which was pointed toward the door as he approached it.

I could hear my heat beating as I waited for the chief to come back out, or worse yet, hear the sound of a gun going off.

When Officer Grant showed up on foot beside my window, I nearly had a heart attack.

"Where did you come from?" I asked him, trying to catch my breath.

"I parked in front of Grace's place," he said. "Where's the chief?" Officer Grant asked as he looked around for his boss.

"He's inside alone."

"Wait here," Grant said, and then he approached the house himself.

Four minutes later, the two men came out together, but their guns weren't holstered, and their flashlights were still emitting a pair of blinding lights. They both nodded in my direction as the chief beckoned me over to them, so I got out of the Jeep and approached them.

"We're going to take a quick sweep of the park," Chief Martin said. "But before we do, we want to make sure that you're safe. Go inside and lock the door behind you. Suzanne, don't let anyone in until we come back. That's an order."

"That's not going to be a problem," I said as I hurried back to my Jeep, started it, and then quickly pulled it into my parking space. After that, it was a quick sprint to my front door. I couldn't wait to obey the last part of that order, though I normally didn't take well to getting instructions from anyone, let alone the chief of police. After I deadbolted the front door, I finally allowed myself a second to catch my breath. It appeared that I was safe, at least for the moment. After I took a second to collect myself, I looked around the entire house, but nothing seemed out of place. I certainly didn't own anything valuable, so why had someone gone to the trouble of breaking in? Had they actually broken anything, though? I looked at the lock, but it appeared to be undamaged. If that were the case, then how had they gotten in? Was it possible that I'd forgotten to lock the front door on my way out after all? No, I distinctly remembered bolting it in place behind me as I'd left. If they hadn't gotten in that way, then how had they gained access? I looked around a little more thoroughly, and that's when I noticed that it was cooler in Momma's bedroom than it should have been. Pulling the curtain aside, I saw that one window pane was neatly punched out, allowing someone access into my home.

I was still studying the broken window when the two police officers started knocking on the front door. I opened it for them after they both identified themselves, and then I said, "I found out how he got in," leading them to the broken glass.

"It looks like you surprised someone in the middle of a burglary attempt," the chief said. "Somebody must have known your schedule at the donut shop and figured that you wouldn't be home. Why *are* you here at this time of morning, anyway?"

"Emma and Sharon had things under control, so I decided

to come home and take a nap before I went to collect Jake, not that there's any chance of *that* happening now."

"Suzanne, if you'd like, I can patch that window for you until you get it replaced," the chief said.

"Need any help with it, Chief?" Officer Grant asked him.

"Thanks for offering, but I really need you out on patrol," he said.

"Happy to do it," Officer Grant said, and then he winked at me before he left. "Don't worry, Suzanne. They won't come back again anytime soon."

"I hope you're right," I said, not even thinking about that possibility before he'd mentioned it.

Once Officer Grant was gone, the chief said, "I know that there's some plywood around here somewhere. I remember seeing it when we were packing your mother's things."

"Chief, she doesn't have to know about this, does she?" I asked him.

"Suzanne, your mother and I don't keep secrets from each other. As a matter of fact, I called her the second we hung up when you dialed 911. Actually, I'm a little surprised that she's not here yet."

At that moment, I heard the front door open. "Suzanne, Phillip, where are you?"

I had to smile, even though I had little reason to at the moment. I hadn't wanted my mother to worry about me, but now that she was at the cottage, I had to admit that I felt a lot better about her being around again.

"I never should have moved out in the first place," Momma said once the two of us were seated on the sofa in the living room. The police chief was busy patching the window, and we'd decided to give him some room to work, so we'd moved out into the living room.

"That's crazy," I said. "If you'd been here, this could have ended up being much worse than it turned out to be."

"But Suzanne, if I'd been here, no one would have dared try to rob the place."

I laughed a little softly before I replied. “Momma, nobody knows how fierce you are more than I do, but you probably wouldn’t discourage a thief from hitting this place if they’d already made up their mind that we were a target.”

“Nevertheless, I’m honestly beginning to regret my decision to leave. The three of us would have found a way to cohabitate.”

I didn’t even want to think about the image of Momma, Jake, and me living under the same roof. Sometimes the cottage felt cramped with just my mother and me. Adding my boyfriend to the mix would have just served to escalate things that much more. “Jake’s going to be here in a few hours,” I said. “Do you honestly believe that I’m not safe with him, even if he does have a wounded arm?”

“No, I know that he’ll take good care of you,” she conceded.

“And I’ll take good care of him, too,” I added softly.

“Of course you will,” she said softly. “I know I’m being silly, but I’m your mother, so I’m allowed.”

“Then you’re not moving back in?” I asked her gently.

She laughed, which was a very good sign. “I’m not out of here for a day yet and already you’re trying to keep me away.”

“You know better than that,” I said as I hugged her. “You’re welcome anytime.”

“I appreciate that,” she replied.

Chief Martin came out of the bedroom with a smile on his face. “That should hold until you can get it fixed. It won’t be long, because I called a friend of mine. I hope you don’t mind. He’ll be here in two hours.”

I glanced at the clock and saw that it would give me until seven to take a quick nap. “I appreciate you taking care of it for me. Thanks.”

“Thank you, Phillip,” Momma added.

He smiled. “You’re both most welcome. It was my pleasure. In the meantime, I’m going to hang around until he gets here.”

"I'll keep you company," Momma said.

"As much as I appreciate both of your offers, I'm going to be fine on my own now." I said it firmly, without a hint of wavering in my voice.

Chief Martin started to say something in rebuttal when Momma shook her head slightly. He clammed right up as Momma stood. "We understand," my mother said. "You'll call if you need us though, right?"

"Of course I will," I said.

"Let's go, Phillip," Momma said firmly.

"But…"

My mother no more than glanced at him, but the police chief decided that whatever he'd been about to say wasn't going to be worth it. "I'll be nearby if you need me, Suzanne," he said as they started to go.

"Thanks, and thank you for coming so promptly."

"Happy to do it," he said, and then both of them were gone.

I started up the stairs for my nap, but I wasn't sure that I wanted to be so far away from the door in case something else happened. After grabbing a blanket from the closet, I decided it might be best just to curl up on the couch, positive that I wouldn't be able to nod off after what had just happened.

It turned out that yet again, I was wrong.

The next thing I knew someone was banging on the front door, announcing himself as the window guy there to fix things up for me.

It appeared that I'd managed to fall asleep after all.

Half an hour later, the window was as good as new. When I'd tried to pay the man for his work, he shook off my request. "I appreciate the offer, but it's already been taken care of."

"Nonsense. I can't let the chief pay for my window," I said.

"He didn't," the repairman answered with a smile. "Your mother took care of it. That's why I was so late. The two of them couldn't stop arguing over who was going to pick up the tab. I offered to let them both pay me, but my suggestion was blatantly ignored," he said with a grin. "Anyway, you're as good as new."

I thanked him and let him out. As I did, my cell phone rang.

What a surprise. It was Jake!

"Hey, I didn't expect to hear from you until this afternoon," I said as I locked the front door.

"I've got great news. At least I hope it's great news."

"Tell me," I said, not even trying to kill my smile. His good mood was infectious, though I didn't know how he could be so cheerful after being shot so recently.

"My doctor came by early, and he's discharging me right now. I know we agreed that you could come by and pick me up later, but is there any chance that you can leave the donut shop and come get me now?"

"I'm on my way, if you don't mind that I smell like donuts."

He laughed. "Mind it? Are you crazy? That's just an added bonus, if you ask me."

"Then I'll see you soon," I said. After splashing a little water on my face and running a comb through my hair, I was out the door.

It felt odd knowing that when I came back to the cottage, I'd have Jake with me.

A part of me was nervous, but mostly I just couldn't wait to have him there.

I was surprised to find Officer Terry Hanlan with Jake when I went to his room at the hospital. The state police inspectors were clearly conferring about something in earnest, and both men had serious expressions on their faces. Jake was still on the bed, but he was sitting up, fully clothed and obviously ready to get out of there.

"Hey, guys. Am I interrupting something?" I asked as I knocked on the door.

"No, I was just leaving," Terry said. On his way out, he paused beside me and added, "Take good care of him, Suzanne."

"I'll do the best that I can," I said.

"I'm sure that you will. I'll see you soon," Terry added, but he was gone before I had a chance to ask him what he'd meant by that.

Jake forced a smile when I looked at him. "You're a sight for sore eyes. I'm really glad that you could make it, but I'm beginning to feel bad about making you abandon your donut shop in the middle of a workday."

"I was already home," I admitted. "Sharon and Emma had things under control. When I realized that they didn't need me, I took off. What did Terry mean when he said that he'd see me soon?"

"We can talk about that later." Jake stared at me a moment before he spoke again. "What happened, Suzanne? You're not having second thoughts about having me come stay at the cottage, are you?"

"Of course not," I said. "It's going to be wonderful having you there."

"Then what is it? I know you well enough to know that something's not right."

I shrugged. "This is clearly one of the downsides of dating a police inspector," I said. "I can't get away with anything."

"Talk to me."

"Only if you agree to tell me what you and Terry were discussing earlier," I countered. I didn't want to bring up the break-in before we had a chance to get settled in, but if I was going to have to share my bad news, then so was Jake. We needed to make a few new rules right out of the gate if we were going to make this thing work.

"Tell you what. Let's save it all for the ride back to April Springs, shall we?"

"You've got yourself a deal," I said as I grabbed his bag. "Now, what do we have to do to break you out of this joint?"

"Everything's already been taken care of," he said. "I've

just been waiting for you."

"Not long, I hope," I said as he started to get up.

"No, not long at all."

"Just what do you think you're doing, young man?" a nurse asked Jake as she poked her head into his room.

"I'm breaking out, Sally," he said with a grin.

"Not without one last ride, you're not," she said in a commanding voice. "Sit down, mister. I'll be back in two minutes with your wheelchair."

"That's ridiculous. I don't need it," Jake protested.

"Inspector, what you think you need and what you're going to get just may be two entirely different things," she said to him, and then she turned to me. "Are you strong enough to keep this man in line while he's recovering?"

"You'd better believe it. He doesn't stand a chance," I said with a smile.

The nurse sized me up for a moment, and then she nodded her approval. "No, I suppose he doesn't. Don't let him overdo it, and make sure he keeps that arm in a sling at all times. Are we clear?"

"I understand completely," I said.

"Hey, I'm right here, people," Jake said. "Need I remind you both that I've been taking care of myself long before I met either one of you?"

"Isn't he cute?" Sally asked. "I love it when they think they know better than we do. You and I know differently, don't we?"

"We do what we can," I said.

"Can I please just get out of here?" Jake asked, clearly frustrated by our lack of progress in leaving.

"Since you said please, I'll go get your ride," the nurse said cheerfully.

Once Sally was gone, Jake looked at me sullenly. "You're not going to try to order me around once we get to the cottage, are you?"

"As long as you do as you've been told, we'll be fine," I said. "Otherwise, I'm not making any promises."

"I was afraid of that," he said, a little more sullenly than I would have liked. "Suzanne, I truly appreciate you taking care of me, but you should know from the start that I won't be babied. Can you accept that?"

"I won't baby you, Jake, but you have to let me do my job."

"What job is that?" he asked me with a grin.

"It's mostly just making sure that you get better, and that means that you need to take care of yourself and not overdo it."

"I'll try, but I can't make any promises." He took a deep breath, and then let it out slowly. "To be honest with you, I've been used to doing things my own way for a long time, and I have always had a problem with authority figures."

"Why on earth did you ever become a cop, then?" I asked out of honest curiosity.

"The truth is that I've always hated bullies. Plus, I've been pretty good at solving puzzles since I was a kid. It seemed like a perfect match for me, once I learned to hold my tongue when I had to."

"I see where that could be a valuable skill to have," I said with the ghost of a grin.

"Well, it has been so far," he replied.

Sally returned with the wheelchair, and Jake said in mock exasperation, "Finally."

She pretended to back out of the room. "If this isn't a good time for you, I can always come back after my break."

"No, this is perfect," Jake said quickly.

"I thought it might be. Now, let's get you loaded up."

"I meant what I said before. I can walk just fine, Sally. You said so yourself this morning."

"Officer Bishop, once you leave these grounds, you can dance away for all I care, but until then, I'm rolling you to the curb."

"I might as well give up then," he said. "Let's not dawdle, though."

Sally was as good as her word. She rolled Jake through the

hospital and out the front door. The nurse waited for me as I retrieved my Jeep and pulled it around to pick my boyfriend up. Jake stood on his own, not without a bit of a bobble, but I wasn't about to help him into the Jeep, and neither was Sally. Once he was safely belted into the passenger seat, Sally leaned forward and patted his hand as she said tenderly, "Take care of yourself, and try not to get shot anymore, okay?"

"I'll do my best."

I started the Jeep, but Sally said, "Hang on a second before you go, Suzanne." She walked around to my side and handed me a sheaf of papers. "You need to read these when you get him to where you're going. Everything's laid out there, but if you have any questions, don't hesitate to call me, day or night." She handed me a slip of paper as well. "I don't usually do this, but this is my cell phone number. I'm available to you around the clock, so don't be afraid to get in touch, okay?"

"Thanks," I said as I took the number from her. "You don't have to do this, you know?"

"My dad was a cop," she said softly. "I really do."

"Got it," I said.

As Sally walked back to the curb, I asked Jake, "So, are you ready for your big adventure?"

"You bet I am. How about you?"

"Well, if nothing else, it should be a unique experience for both of us," I said as I started the Jeep and drove off. I could see Sally still standing there waving as we left the parking lot, and I noticed Jake smiling softly back at her as he returned her wave.

I just hoped that I could do half the job that Sally had done for him. If I could manage that, I knew that Jake would be all right.

Chapter 7

Jake had his window open, and he breathed the fresh air in deeply as we started to drive. "I didn't think I'd ever get out of there. Can you smell that?" he asked me.

I took a whiff of the air. "I'm not sure what you mean. I don't smell anything out of the ordinary."

"That's because you're not sitting in *my* seat. Over here, it smells exactly like freedom to me."

We drove a little more before I finally decided that it was time to break the happy silence of the ride. "We both know that we can't keep avoiding it, Jake. We need to talk before we get back to April Springs. So, who wants to go first?"

"You should go ahead," Jake said. "Mine's probably nothing."

"So is mine," I said.

He wasn't about to budge, though. "Suzanne, I still want you to go first."

"Fine." I took a deep breath, and then I said, "There was a break-in at the cottage this morning."

"What! What happened? Are you okay? Why am I just hearing about this now?" I hadn't wanted to upset him, but it was understandable enough. It was time now for me to downplay it as much as I could. After all, I didn't want it to ruin the rest of the day for us.

"Take it easy, Jake. I wasn't even there when it happened, so I'm fine. I came home early after our break at the donut shop, and I found the front door ajar."

"You didn't go in by yourself, did you?" he asked me, clearly worried about the possibility that I'd acted rashly. I couldn't even blame him for jumping to that particular conclusion, since I hadn't always acted in the past in the most rational way.

"No, I did what I was supposed to do. I dialed 911, and Chief Martin came almost immediately." I hesitated telling him the rest of it, but if I expected full disclosure from him, I was going to have to do the same thing myself. "There's something else that you should know. After I'd been there about a minute, I saw someone running away from the house."

"Did you get a good look at them? Were you able to give Martin a description?"

"It was too dark," I admitted. "I couldn't even tell if it was a man or a woman, to be honest with you."

"Did he find anything when he got there?" Jake asked, his voice calming down a little as he spoke.

"No, evidently whoever broke in didn't have time to steal anything. Chief Martin and Officer Grant checked the house thoroughly, and they even checked the park, but whoever did it was long gone. The chief thinks that it was just someone who saw us moving Momma out and thought the place would be ripe for a burglary. The window where they broke in has been fixed, and everything is as good as new." I took another deep breath, and then I said, "I would have told you about it sooner, but I didn't want to worry you. I knew that you should be aware of what was going on, though."

"I appreciate your candor," Jake said, but there was a hint of hesitation in his voice as he said it. "You're right. This is something that I need to know. Suzanne, before I tell you my news, it's important that you don't automatically jump to the conclusion that the two things are related, okay?"

I eased up on the gas pedal as I glanced over at him. "I refuse to make any promises until I hear your news. What is it that you have to tell me?"

"Evidently the guy I shot wasn't working alone," Jake said guardedly. "Evidently Jeffrey Wade Monroe had a partner in crime, a guy named Harry Rusk that we didn't know about. That's what Terry was telling me about this morning when you showed up."

"Do you think that he might have been the one who broke into my place?" I asked.

"Suzanne, according to federal agents up north, there are reports that Rusk was spotted outside a gas station in

Pennsylvania this morning. He couldn't have been the one who broke into your place."

"What if the reports are wrong, though?" I asked. "You said yourself that eyewitnesses are usually the worst kind of evidence you can have."

"Think about it. Even if Rusk were still in the area, how could he possibly know that I'm going to be staying with you? And even if, by some miracle, he was able to find that out, why break in before I get there? It just doesn't make any sense."

"I guess not," I said, a little mollified by the logic of his argument, "but that still doesn't mean that I'm not going to worry that they're connected somehow."

"You should really think about saving your worries for things that might actually happen," he said.

"Is there anything else that you're not telling me?" I asked him. "Let's lay it all out on the table before we get home." Jake looked at me in surprise as I said the last word, and I had to back up fast to explain myself. "I didn't mean that it was your home, though I want you to think of it that way for at least the next month. It's just an expression, Jake, so don't read anything into it."

"I didn't say a word," Jake replied coolly.

"You didn't have to. Your expression said enough."

"You shouldn't read too much into it, Suzanne. I'm just a little tired, that's all," Jake said. "So don't take anything I say or do too personally. I just want to get to the cottage and stretch out on the couch."

"You can use the bed downstairs if you'd like," I said. "The master suite is all yours for the duration of your stay."

"No, if you don't mind, I'll just rest a little in the living room. I'd feel a little lazy taking a nap so soon after getting up."

"But snoozing on the couch is okay, right?" I asked him with a grin.

"Hey, it's the average American male's favorite pastime, isn't it?" he asked with a smile of his own. I was glad that we'd cleared the air. At least now we both knew what we were dealing with.

"Maybe for some average males it is, but we both know that you are anything but average," I said. "But if it makes you feel any better, you can doze off wherever you'd like, as long as you promise to take it easy for at least the next couple of weeks."

He moved his slinged arm a bit. "You're not going to have to worry about that. Up until now, I've used my left hand mainly for holding a knife and a little typing. It's going to take me some time to get used to not using my right hand for everything."

"Don't worry. I'll be there to help you until you get the hang of it," I said.

"I know, and I greatly appreciate it."

We finally made it to the cottage, and I was beginning to feel better about everything, until I noticed the squad car parked in the driveway. I hoped that it was just Chief Martin paying us a social call, but somehow I doubted it.

It turned out that I was right to be concerned about the reason for his visit, much to my regret.

Jake spoke up before I had a chance to once we were all standing by my Jeep. "Is there news on Rusk, Chief?"

"Who's Rusk?" Chief Martin asked.

"It turns out that Monroe had a partner we didn't know about," Jake explained. "In case you didn't know, Monroe is the guy I shot."

"I know that much, at least," the chief said, and then he looked at Jake. "Do your people have any idea on where this Rusk character might be right now?"

"He was supposedly spotted up north this morning," I said.

"That's probably exactly where he is, too," the police chief said. "I wouldn't worry about him too much if I were you."

"But we all know that sometimes eyewitness reports can be wrong," I answered.

"That's a fair point. Jake, I'll need to know more about this Rusk character if there's one chance in a hundred he might show up around here," the police chief said.

"You can talk to a friend of mine in the department," Jake said, and he gave him Terry's name and phone number.

"If that's not why you're here, then what's the real reason for this visit?" I asked. "I kind of doubt you're a one-man welcoming committee."

"Heather Masterson escaped from the hospital last night," Chief Martin said tersely.

"The woman who poisoned her aunt and then came after Suzanne? How did she manage to escape?" Jake asked. "Besides, I thought she was in prison, not a hospital."

"She was," the chief explained, "but she got into a fight with another inmate and had to be transferred so she could recover from her injuries. Heather was just about to be sent back when she made her break yesterday afternoon about the time we were moving your mother into her new place."

"And now you think she might be coming after me to get revenge for my help in putting her away," I said. "Do you think she's the one who broke into the cottage this morning?"

"I don't know," the chief said. "I'm not ready to jump to any conclusions at the moment, but I thought you should at least know what happened. Your mother is worried about you staying here; that's for sure."

"Don't forget that Suzanne is not alone. *I'm* with her," Jake said. "She'll be fine."

"No offense intended," Chief Martin replied, "but I'm not exactly sure that you're going to offer her much protection. With that busted wing, how much security are you going to be able to offer Suzanne?"

"Don't worry about us. I can shoot with my left hand if I need to," Jake said.

"I don't doubt it, but Dorothea would still feel better if you both stayed with her until Heather is caught."

I shook my head at the suggestion. "Tell Momma that we said thanks, but we're staying right here."

"Suzanne, it might not be such a bad idea after all," Jake said. "The chief makes a good point. We both know that I'm not one hundred percent, and I won't be for awhile."

"Between the two of us, I know that we can handle anything that comes our way," I said, and then I turned back to the chief. "Thanks for stopping by, but we've got to move Jake in now."

Chief Martin clearly didn't know how to react to our refusal. I didn't envy him the conversation he'd be having soon with my mother, and I knew that I hadn't heard the end of this from her either, but for now, I was standing firm. "Can I at least give you a hand?" he offered.

I handed him Jake's bag to show that there were no hard feelings. "Go on and take it into the master bedroom," I said. "We'll be along in a second."

"You agree with me about this, right?" I asked Jake as soon as Chief Martin was inside.

"Suzanne, whatever you want to do is fine by me. I just don't want anything to happen to you on my watch because I was too weak to protect you."

"This isn't your watch, and I don't need protecting," I reminded him. "You are here to recover from your injury, not to keep me safe. Do you understand that?"

"Why can't I do both?" he asked me with a crooked grin.

"How about if we take care of each other?" I suggested.

"That's even better."

"So then, we're staying right where we are, right?" I asked him.

"Until you tell me differently. But we both need to be especially vigilant, Suzanne, and that means no door or window goes unlocked, and one of us doesn't go anywhere without telling the other. Can you agree to that?"

I thought about the times I might need to run to the store or the pharmacy, and how inconvenient it would be to check in with him every time I had to step outside. "What if you're asleep?"

"Then you wake me up. If you can't agree to do this, then I

can't stay here."

If Jake was bluffing, then he was better at it than I ever hoped to be. "Okay. I get it. I agree."

"Then let's get me moved in," he said with a smile.

"Do you need a hand with the steps?"

"I got shot in the arm, not the leg," Jake said as he put a hand on the railing.

"I know that, but you haven't spent that much time on your feet the past few days. If you want to put your arm around me when you walk up the steps, I'm okay with that."

"Suzanne, I don't hate the idea of putting my arm around you, but it won't be to steady my step, I can promise you that."

"Easy there, tiger. You need to recuperate first."

"If that's not incentive enough for me to get better, then I don't know what is," he said with a smile.

I ended up steadying him a little after all as he made his way up the short steps, but neither one of us commented on it. I was going to have to let him go at his own pace and not be overprotective. Not only was that what Jake wanted, but he needed it as well. The man was stubborn, willful, and fiercely independent, three traits that I loved about him the most, but it wasn't going to make him easy to live with, especially given his injury.

"I put your bag on the bed," the police chief said as Jake and I walked into the house.

"Thanks," Jake said as he patted his pants pocket with his good hand. "I'd tip you right now if I could, but my wallet's on the other side of my pants, and with this stupid sling, I can't get to it."

"That's okay. You can owe me," the chief said with a grin. "I'm proud to know you, Officer Bishop."

The sentiment caught Jake off-guard. "Right back at you, Chief," he said.

After the police chief was gone, Jake asked me, "What was that all about?"

"Haven't you been reading the papers? It turns out that you're a hero."

Jake frowned at that, and then he said, "Don't you start with me."

"Don't worry. You won't have to hear me ever say anything like that," I promised him.

Jake shrugged. "Well, maybe a little adoration would be in order every now and then."

I laughed, happy that he'd survived getting shot and was now here with me. "You can't have it both ways, buddy."

"Then I'll take you just as you are right now."

"That's convenient, but that's what you were going to get whether you like it or not. Now, who's hungry?"

"I'm starving," Jake said. "They wouldn't give me anything like real food at the hospital, no matter how much I begged for it."

"We'll see if we can fix that, then. What would you like?"

"Well, I'd *like* a steak, but since I can't cut it without your help, I'll take a sandwich instead."

I led him into the kitchen and opened the freezer. Momma might have moved out, but she'd left a ton of food behind. "How about pot roast and cooked veggies?"

"You don't have to go to that much trouble for me on the first day," Jake said.

"What trouble? I just have to thaw it out and it will be ready to eat. We're talking leftovers here, nothing made from scratch."

"Then pot roast sounds great. I'm going to have to start that exercise program early though, if I still want to be able to fit into my clothes when my arm heals."

"We can walk in the park together," I said. "It will be fun, but you have to promise me that you'll stop and rest whenever you get tired."

"It's a deal, but for now, I think I'll stick with walking to the bedroom and back. How long is it going to take to be ready to eat?"

"I can give you something to snack on in the meantime if

you'd like," I said.

"I was thinking more along the lines of a quick nap on the couch," Jake admitted.

"Take all of the time you need," I said. "This can wait."

"Don't let me sleep too long. Wake me when it's ready," Jake said as he headed for the living room.

"I don't think so. Sorry, but you need your rest. You'll wake up in your own good time when you get hungry enough, so don't expect *me* to be your alarm clock."

"You're one tough cookie, do you know that?"

"I've heard it a time or two," I said. "Have a good nap."

I put the pot roast and fixings in the oven and let the temperature rise gradually as it started to heat. I wasn't in the kitchen three minutes when I peeked in at Jake to check on him.

He was already sound asleep.

It looked as though he might be awhile, so I grabbed a piece of pie from the fridge to hold me until my recovering boyfriend woke up.

All in all, it was a pretty fantastic way to wait for him. After I finished it, I cleaned up a little in the kitchen. As I worked, I couldn't help wondering if Momma was right. Should Jake and I risk staying at the cottage while two maniacs were on the loose, both of whom wanted to cause us pain? It made perfect sense for us to go where we couldn't be found, but I just couldn't bring myself to abandon this house just because someone might want to harm me there. This was home, and I wasn't going to let anyone take that from me, no matter how much sense evacuating might make. Besides, I had a great deal of faith in our ability to take care of ourselves.

I just hoped that I wasn't wrong, because if I were, it might end up being a fatal, and final, mistake.

Chapter 8

So, the cop had lived after all. Normally I wasn't all that big on revenge, but this guy Bishop had ruined our plans, and I wasn't about to let him get away with it.

Sure, he'd taken a bullet to the arm, but he was going to live, which was more than I could say for Morton.

How long Bishop kept breathing was something else altogether.

In the end, it wasn't that hard to find him. He was shacking up with his girlfriend, a donut maker named Suzanne Hart. They were both in April Springs, and that was all that I needed to know.

Chapter 9

Soon after I finished rinsing my pie plate, there was a tap on the kitchen window that nearly scared me to death. When I looked up from where I was sitting at the table, I was relieved to see Momma standing outside, but when I noticed who was with her, I was startled yet again. What was our mayor doing with Momma? Then I saw the shotgun in his hands, and I was even more disturbed. I went to the front door to let them in and saw that Jake was quietly snoozing on the couch. The day must have taken a lot out of him, and I was glad that he'd been able to fall asleep so quickly, and so soundly. I slipped outside and gently shut the door behind me. "He's sleeping," I said softly, even though I knew that there was no way that Jake could hear us now as long as we kept our voices at a reasonable level.

"That's good for him," Momma said. "He needs all of the rest that he can get right now."

I ignored her for the moment and turned to my friend, the mayor. "George, not that I'm not happy to see you, but what exactly are you doing here with a shotgun?"

He frowned at my mother. "You didn't tell her, Dorothea?"

"There hasn't been time," Momma said. "While my daughter and I talk, why don't you take a walk around the park?"

"With this in my hands?" the mayor asked as he held out his gun. "I might scare a few constituents if they see that I'm armed."

"Lean it over there against the house, then," she said, and George started to do just that, but then he must have thought better of it. "Maybe I'll just keep it with me after all."

"That might be for the best," Momma said.

As George left, I turned to my mother and asked, "What exactly is going on here?"

Momma just shrugged. "You wouldn't leave the cottage.

What other choice did we have?"

"Just because we wouldn't relocate, you enlisted the mayor to stand guard?"

"Oh, it's not just the mayor," Momma said. "He just has the first shift. Phillip is taking over in four hours, and then young Officer Grant will be here."

This was too much. "Momma, I know that the chief loves you, but he can't make a police officer stand guard over us. Can he?"

"As a matter of fact, Stephen volunteered for the duty, as did George and Phillip. Suzanne, you'll have someone out here around the clock until the need is no longer there."

"They can't work long shifts standing guard here," I protested. "It's not fair to them. After all, these men have lives of their own."

"The three I mentioned are just doing it in the evenings and early morning hours. Tomorrow morning, a very nice police inspector named Terry Hanlan has volunteered to watch over you from nine AM to seven PM. I believe the two of you have already met."

"We have," I said. "Are the state police taking the threat that credibly?"

Momma frowned. "Evidently not. Terry is taking some personal time to ensure your safety. He'll be here during the day for the next five days before his vacation time is gone. Since he can't watch over you both twenty-four hours a day, a handful of other men in this community have volunteered their services."

"I hate the idea of anyone losing sleep because of me."

Momma patted my hand. "Suzanne, as much as they all care for you, you aren't the only reason they're all willing to lose out on some sleep. Jake has made quite a few friends in April Springs during his time with you."

"I realize that, but it's all just a little too much," I said.

"Then move somewhere else until things settle down," Momma said. "Problem solved."

"Sorry, but you know that I just can't do that."

"I understand completely," she said, "but this is the next best solution."

"I'm still not sure that's true. I need to talk to Jake about this," I said as I started back inside.

"Suzanne, let the poor man sleep. He's been through a lot lately, and he doesn't need to worry about this until he wakes up."

"You're right," I said. "Okay. Thanks for arranging this."

She looked surprised by the compliment. "My dear darling daughter, I had nothing to do with it. This was George and Phillip's idea, and when Stephen found out what they were doing, he insisted on taking a shift himself."

"That's very kind of them all," I said, more than a little touched by the very real gestures of my friends.

"What can I say? You are loveable enough in your own right, and this town has grown to accept Jake as one of their own. After all, he put his life on the line and was wounded for it. We will not stand by and watch either one of you put in danger now. You can sleep peacefully tonight knowing that good men are watching over you."

"I'm not so sure how good I'll sleep, but I do appreciate what they're doing."

"No way were we going to just stand idly by," George said as he approached us coming from the park. "The perimeter is all clear."

"Sometimes I forget that you were once a cop," I said with a smile.

"Once a cop, always a cop," George said. "The fact that I'm no longer on active police duty doesn't mean a thing. I might be the mayor around here, but I won't always be. Somehow it's not in my blood the way police work is."

"I think being mayor is more a part of you than you realize," Momma said.

"If it is, I only have you to blame for it," George said with a smile. He was right, too. Momma had orchestrated a write-in vote for his candidacy, mostly because she didn't want the job she was running for herself, but she couldn't stand the thought of her other opponent taking over, either. Her decision might have been self-serving, but it had been a good one for April Springs nonetheless.

"Well, I have things to tend to," Momma said. "Suzanne, you are in good hands."

"I know that," I said as I hugged her. "Thanks."

"For what? I told you that I wasn't involved in this."

"I'm not so sure that I believe you, but that's okay," I said with a grin.

Momma wanted to smile back, but I saw her stifle it at the last instant. "You know, you always were a stubborn child."

"Like mother, like daughter, I suppose," I said as I laughed.

After she was gone, George pulled a porch chair over by the door and sat down. "You know, there aren't many folks who would talk to your mother like that and get away with it, Suzanne."

"I like to think of it as a daughter's prerogative," I replied. I glanced in through the window and saw that Jake was still sound asleep, so I pulled up another chair and joined George at his post.

"It's okay if you want to go back inside. You know that you don't have to stand watch with me," he said.

"I don't have to, but I'd like a little company, if you don't mind."

"In that case, you're more than welcome to join me," he said. The shotgun was across his lap, and though we were chatting warmly, I noticed that his gaze never stopped surveying the land around us.

"George, are you really expecting whoever broke in here to come back? It was probably just a random robbery attempt."

"It very well might have been, but it's still prudent for us to keep our vigil. There are some very bad people out there, Suzanne."

"Are you talking about Heather or this man Rusk?" I asked him softly.

"Yes to both of them," George answered with the hint of a

grin. "Maybe even a third person, if neither one of them broke into your place this morning."

"I can't imagine Heather coming after me if she finally managed to escape," I said. "After all, I wasn't the one who arrested her. Maybe Chief Martin should be the one who's afraid."

"Come on, Suzanne. We both know that you were instrumental in catching her. It wouldn't surprise me one bit that she might fixate on you, and from what I understand, prison time is slow time. She's had a lot of time to think about you while she was locked up."

The thought that a killer would obsess about me behind bars gave me the chills, and frankly, it was something I'd never really thought about before. Once Grace and I caught our suspects, I tended to forget about them. Something else occurred to me just then. "George, you were helping me work on the investigation when I caught Heather. What makes you think that you're not a target, too?"

He smiled as he said, "Honestly, I'm not worried about it, because if I am on her hit list, then I'm a target that knows how to shoot back." He patted his shotgun affectionately as he said it.

"Do you think Grace is in danger as well?"

"I don't think so," George said, "but we're keeping a bit of an eye on her as well."

That definitely made me feel better. "Does she have a guard around the clock, too?"

"Nothing that intense," George said, "but then again, she wasn't the focus of Heather's ire, either, and don't forget, she doesn't have anything to do with Rusk."

"To tell you the truth, he's the one who really scares me," I said.

"That's probably a healthy attitude to have about him," George admitted. "I spoke with Terry Hanlan over the phone before I came over here, and he told me a few chilling things that I don't care to repeat."

Wow. If something the state policeman had said chilled

George, I wasn't sure that I wanted to know about it, either. "Jake doesn't think Rusk will come after him."

George just shrugged. "Even if that's so, what we're doing here is important. We want to show you and Jake our appreciation, and if it means a few lost hours of sleep, we can all live happily enough with that." He paused, and then grinned a little. "Besides, the older I get, the less sleep I seem to need."

I wasn't sure that I liked being protected like some kind of princess, but I did appreciate knowing that these men cared about Jake and me. "How about some coffee while you're standing guard?"

"I wouldn't say no to a cup," George said with a smile.

I'd noticed a few pies in the fridge Momma had made. "And maybe a slice of pie, too?"

"Suzanne, if you take that good care of us, none of us may ever leave."

"I'll take that as a yes," I said. "I'll be back in a few minutes."

"Take your time. I'm not going anywhere."

I made the coffee and cut the mayor a healthy slice of pie while it was brewing. As I carried them both to the door, Jake surprised me by sitting up. "You can eat that right here as long as you get some for me," he said as he sat up. "I'm awake."

"As a matter of fact, this isn't for me," I said.

"How did you know that I'd want some?" he asked with a grin as he held his hands out to me.

"Sorry, but it's not for you, either."

Jake looked puzzled. "If it's not for me and it's not for you, then may I ask who gets it?"

"The mayor is out front with his shotgun," I explained. "He's on guard duty."

I expected Jake to protest, but he just nodded instead. "That's good. I was hoping that someone would step up."

"You're not upset?" I asked him.

"No. As a matter of fact, I'm kind of surprised that my boss didn't assign us some men himself. I think he's still a little miffed at me for getting shot."

"How can he be mad about that?" I asked incredulously.

Jake tried to shrug, but the sling wouldn't let him do it very easily. "He's lost a valuable asset for the next four weeks. Why wouldn't he be unhappy about it?"

"But that happened in the line of duty," I protested. I was getting to like his boss less and less, and I'd only met the man once.

"Either way, it's good to have someone watching over us while I heal. I hope George isn't going to stay out there all night by himself."

"He's not," I said. "Chief Martin is taking a shift, and then Officer Grant is going to come by until Terry Hanlan checks in."

Jake looked surprised to hear his old friend's name. "Has Terry been assigned to us? I knew that he said that he'd stop by to check on me later, but I didn't think it was going to be like this."

"No, evidently he's taking some leave time to be here during the day. Jake, I know that he said you were friends, but it's awfully generous of him to give up his vacation for us."

My boyfriend looked a little uncomfortable when I said that, and I knew that there was more to the story than I knew. "Why would he do that?" I asked. "What is it that you're not telling me?"

"It's probably because he's under the mistaken impression that I saved his life once," Jake finally admitted.

"Did you?" I asked.

"Shouldn't you be delivering that coffee to George before it gets cold?" Jake asked.

"Sure, I'll do it in a second. First, I want to hear what happened."

Jake rubbed his face with his good hand, and then he stared at me. "You're not going to let up until I tell you, are you?"

I grinned at him. "You know me too well."

"Fine. We were on a stakeout together, and he went to check on our suspect, against my advice. When he didn't come back right away, I decided to see what was going on. I snuck around and saw that our guy had a gun to Terry's head. I managed to distract him a little, and Terry got out of it okay after all."

"How exactly did you distract him, Jake?"

He mumbled something, but I couldn't make it out.

"We both know that I didn't quite catch that. I'm not sure that I was meant to."

"I shot the bad guy in the rear end, okay?" Jake asked. "He dropped the gun, and Terry grabbed him."

"Weren't you risking shooting your partner instead?" I asked him.

"Well, I decided that it was worth a shot, you know?" He smiled a little at that. "No pun intended."

"Was your suspect really a bad guy?"

"Oh, yes. We found drugs and guns out in plain sight. This man needed to be off the streets, and we took care of him. I keep telling Terry that it was nothing, but he still won't let me forget it."

"Jake, he's right. You kind of did save his life."

"I guess if you look at it one way you could say that," he said. "Now will you take that to George?"

"I will, and then I'll be back with yours," I said.

Jake pretended to frown at me. "So you're saying that I'm the one who got shot, and I get served last? That doesn't quite seem fair, does it?"

"Life's not fair, or haven't you heard? Learn to live with it, hero," I said with a smile.

That made him laugh. "Suzanne, I wasn't sure about this arrangement when you first suggested it, but I've got to say, it's good to have you around."

"Right back at you," I said. "I'll just be a second."

I delivered the pie and coffee, which George took gladly as

he leaned his shotgun against the house beside him. I noticed that it was still close enough to reach in case he needed it in a hurry.

"Sorry for the delay," I said.

"No worries. How's he feeling?"

"He's pretending to be grumpy, but I know better," I said.

"That's a good sign, then."

"How's that, George?"

"If Jake's overly polite, that's when you need to start worrying. He's going to be fine. I just know it."

"I think so, too," I said. "I'm sure he'll be out here himself soon to thank you for watching out for us."

"Do me a favor and make him stay on the couch. None of us are doing this for a pat on the back. Tell him I said that, and if he tries to come out here anyway, remind him that I'm the one with the gun." George grinned.

"He's armed, too, you know," I said. It had unsettled me a little when I'd seen Jake's gun on the couch beside him, but it wasn't like a weapon for him. That gun was an extension of who he was, and I was certain that it helped him sleep so comfortably. It was part of who he was, so I was going to have to learn to get over having it around.

"Just tell him not to shoot the messenger, then," George said. "Was he upset when you told him that we were going to be out here all night?"

"I thought he might be, but to be honest with you, he seemed kind of pleased more than anything." I leaned forward and kissed the mayor's cheek, which got a smile from him.

"What was that for?"

"For caring enough to give up what little sleep you get these days," I said.

"Like I said, we're all happy to do it."

When I got back inside the cottage, Jake had shifted around on the couch, sitting up now and resting his slinged arm on a pillow. "Are you comfortable?" I asked him.

"I suppose so." He looked at the arrangement, and then he added a little wistfully, "This is probably as good as it's going to get for awhile."

I glanced at the clock. "Would you like a pill for the pain? You can have one now, if you'd like."

"Let's see how it goes and save it for later," he said. "I might need a little help getting to sleep tonight. Do you know what I'd really like?"

I didn't wait for an answer; I just leaned in and kissed his cheek, too. After all, if it was good enough for George, it was certainly good enough for Jake.

"Sure, that's wonderful and all, but what I was really hoping for was some of your mother's homemade pot roast."

I started to throw a pillow at him, but I quickly changed my mind. If I hit his bandaged arm, I was certain that it could hurt him. Instead, I shifted at the last second, and still holding onto the pillow, I gave him a gentle thump upside his head.

He laughed, surprised that I'd hit him, even so gently. "I probably deserved that, but I am fiercely hungry. Would you like to have some, too?"

"Actually, I'm starving myself, even though I had a snack while you were sleeping," I admitted. "I'll be back shortly."

"Don't be gone too long, and I'm not just saying that because I'm hungry."

Even if that wasn't exactly true, it was still nice to hear.

Chapter 10

Jake had a little trouble cutting the carrots and potatoes with only a fork at first, but I quickly took care of that, portioning out the meal into bite-sized servings that he could handle without any help from me.

He protested after I finished cutting up his meal. "I feel like such a little kid."

"I understand your frustration, but it's just easier this way, don't you think?"

"I suppose so, but that doesn't mean that I have to like it." He frowned at his plate, and then stabbed a small bite.

"It's still better than me feeding you, isn't it?" I asked him.

"Let's face it. Neither one of us is cut out for that," he answered. "You were right. At least I can manage this okay."

He managed just fine with the new arrangement, and I made a mental note to prepare all of his food in more manageable serving sizes before I even brought anything out to him.

After he was finished, he pushed his plate away on its tray. "That was incredible, and not just because I've been eating hospital food for the last twenty-four hours," Jake said as he finished every last bite of the pot roast that I'd given him.

"Would you like more?" I asked as I stood.

"I'd better not," he said as he tried to stretch a little. We'd decided not to move from the couch, since it had taken Jake so long to get himself comfortable. I'd grabbed a pair of the old TV trays we kept in the hall closet and served us both right there.

As I grabbed his tray so I could take it into the kitchen, he said, "I can help with that."

I let go of the tray instantly and sat back down. "Thanks. I'd appreciate that."

I watched him for a full minute as he struggled to pick the tray up, failing miserably the entire time, and doing my best not to laugh. Jake must have sensed it, though, because when he looked over at me, I couldn't contain my grin any longer. "How's that working out for you?"

It was touch and go there for a second, but his good humor finally won out. As Jake slumped back on the couch, he grinned at me. "You have to at least give me points for trying."

"What I need to do is swat you with a newspaper," I said, trying to act sternly but not managing it at all. "Jake, I know that you hate to be taken care of, but you need to find a way to surrender yourself to it. I'm here to help you in any way that I can. Take advantage of that."

"Suzanne, you know that it's hard for me," Jake said softly.

I touched his cheek lightly. "I'm sure that it is. Just remember one thing. I don't love you any less because you happen to need me right now, okay?"

"Okay," he said gently. "I love you, too."

"There, now isn't that better?" I asked as I moved both trays into the kitchen. As I rinsed our dishes and put them in the sink, I called out to him, "Do you have any room left for pie?"

"I'd love some," he said, "but I might explode if I take another bite."

"I understand," I said. "How about if I give you a rain check?"

"That would be perfect," he said. Was his voice a little sleepy as he spoke? I decided to go ahead and do the dishes while he was resting, and in ten minutes, I had the kitchen in perfect shape again.

I started to say something to him as I walked back out into the living room, but I'm glad that I didn't.

He was sound asleep again.

I had a dilemma. Should I wake him so he could move into the bedroom, or just let him sleep where he was? I was leaning toward letting him sleep when he snored loudly for a second, waking himself up as he did.

"Wow, I'm really wiped. Would you mind if I went on to

bed early tonight? It's been a big day."

I glanced at the clock. "Are you kidding? It's past my bedtime as it is."

"But you're not going into work tomorrow, right?" he asked.

"Not a chance. I've got a crack team in place, so why should I?"

"That's the spirit," Jake said as he started to stand, but then he fell back onto the couch again. "How about a little help?"

I helped him up, and he kissed me lightly once he was standing. "You just did that for a kiss, didn't you?" I asked him with a smile.

"I really did need the help. The kiss was just a bonus."

"For me, too," I said. "I laid your pajamas out on the bed. Do you need any help changing?"

"Thanks, but that's one of the few things I can do for myself."

"Okay then. Holler if you need me."

"You can count on it," he said.

I waited five minutes, but when I hadn't heard from him, I decided to see if he needed a hand after all.

Jake was passed out on the bed, sleeping soundly. He'd managed to change into his pajamas, but the effort must have worn him out the rest of the way, since he was still on top of the covers. I took a blanket my grandmother had made and draped it gently over him, being sure not to touch his wounded arm. He rustled a little, but just for a second, before he went fully back to sleep.

I left his door open so I could hear him if he needed me, and then I made the couch up for my night's sleep. It wasn't as comfortable as my bed, but I'd taken many naps on it over the years, so it was like coming back home again when I settled in. I'd decided to forgo jammies of my own tonight, content in sleeping in my jeans and T shirt. It wasn't the most comfortable way to snooze, but I'd manage somehow.

I was sleeping soundly enough, at least I thought so, when

something jarred me awake. There were voices coming from outside! Was it a simple shift in the men guarding us, or was something else happening out there?

I decided that since I was already awake, I'd investigate it for myself. Grabbing my baseball bat from the closet, I looked out the door to see if I could make out what was really going on out there.

"Is something wrong?" Chief Martin asked me as I finally stepped outside.

"We woke you up, didn't we?" George asked.

"No, it's fine. I was already awake." I peered out into the darkness. "Have you seen anything yet?"

"Not a thing worth mentioning," George said as he stretched. "It's been as quiet as a graveyard around here. I was just about ready to head home, unless you need me for something."

"No, you go on. I'm fine. Thanks for coming by."

"Have a good night, then," George said, and then he left the police chief and me.

"Sorry if we were too loud earlier," Chief Martin said.

"It wasn't you." Why did I keep denying the fact that the men had woken me up? Then again, it might not have been them after all. I was used to being up at this time of night, or early morning, and it was clearly going to be a hard habit for me to break.

"Was it because you're used to usually being at work this time of day?"

I nodded, a little surprised that the police chief had come to the same conclusion that I'd just reached myself. "I can't believe that I'm saying this, but I miss being at the donut shop right about now."

"You don't have to explain it to me," the chief said as he took George's chair. "I used to get antsy every time I took a single day of my vacation. I was always chomping at the bit because I couldn't wait to get back on the job."

"But you don't feel that way anymore?" I asked, guessing based on the way he was talking.

"Not nearly as much as I used to. After all, there's only so much I can ask your mother to put up with." He paused, and then the chief added, "Strike that. It's got nothing to do with her, unless you count the fact that I want to be able to spend more time with her than I've been able to do so far."

The chief was in a particularly chatty mood, and I had to wonder if it was due to the time of night, or more correctly, morning. "I'm sure she understands that it's your job. Besides, it's not exactly like she's sitting around on her hands waiting for you to get off work all of the time." I knew how bad that must have sounded to him the moment I'd said it. "Chief, I didn't mean it that way. All I'm saying is that Momma is busy with businesses of her own."

He nodded. "I'm well aware of your mother's responsibilities, but sometimes I think she's as tired of them as I am of mine. She's talked an awful lot lately about selling everything, me retiring, and the two of us just taking off and seeing the world. She doesn't want to die leaving so many things on her list undone, so many places unvisited."

I felt a little wrench in my chest. Momma hadn't breathed a word of those plans to me, and it hurt just a bit, even though she every right to keep these conversations to herself. "Is that what she really wants to do?" I couldn't imagine my daily life without my mother in it, but she had a right to her life just as much as I had a right to mine.

The police chief shook his head, and it was clear that he realized a little too late that he'd upset me. "Don't pay any attention to me, Suzanne. I tend to ramble on sometimes about things I shouldn't talk about. Who knows if any of it is ever going to happen? Dark nights make for dark thoughts sometimes."

"I can relate to that," I said, and then I stopped speaking and listened carefully. Was that a sound coming from inside? I walked to the door, opened it, and then I listened in again. When I didn't hear another sound out of Jake, I continued. "Donut Hearts is brightly lit in the back when Emma and I are working, and there are times that I actually forget what time of day it is until we go outside for our break. But it's especially true when I'm working alone; my mind seems to race in a thousand different directions at the same time."

"Does that include the current nightmare that you're living in?" he asked me.

"Are you kidding? I love having Jake around."

"I didn't mean that, or the fact that your mother moved out, either. I'm talking about something that your mom is scared to death of herself. She worries that I'm going to be killed in the line of duty and leave her before we've had a chance to start our new lives together."

"I admit that I worry about that a lot," I confessed. "As much as I've tried to prepare myself for what just happened, it still doesn't make it any easier on me. I honestly don't know what I'd do if something happened to Jake."

"He's tough, Suzanne. It would take a lot to put him down."

"Don't kid yourself, Chief. He's just as human as everyone else. A great many times, one bullet is all that it takes." I shivered at the thought, hating to even say it aloud.

"I can understand you feeling that way," Chief Martin said, and then we sat in silence for a few moments, each of us left to our own thoughts.

After a while, I asked him softly, "I know you said before that you and Momma have talked about it, but have you ever really *considered* retiring? I'm not asking you for any reason other than my mother has agreed to marry you, and I don't want her to ever have to endure what I've been going through with Jake."

"Honestly, it's all I seem to think about anymore," he said wistfully. "I just don't know how I'd handle life without my work, even with your mother by my side. I've been a cop for as long as I can remember. How do you just stop being one?"

"George managed to do it," I reminded him.

"Sure, but now he's the mayor, so it's not exactly like he

sits home every day sitting by the fire waiting for something to happen."

I stood, but before I went back inside, I said, "I don't want to push you in either direction. You need to make the decision that's right for you. If that's staying on the job, then I'm sure that Momma would understand, and even accept it."

"And if I decide to step down?" he asked.

"I bet she'd be fine with that as well," I replied. "It could be that would be even finer with her," I added with a small smile.

"Maybe so," the police chief said, but it was clear that he wasn't sure either way. At least I'd given him something to think about as he watched over us.

"If it's okay with you, I'm going to try to get a little more sleep before it's time when most normal folks are usually getting up," I said as headed for the door. "Good night, Chief."

"Good night, Suzanne. Jake's a lucky man to have you."

"I think we're lucky to have each other," I said with a smile.

Before I headed back to the couch, I peeked in on Jake and found him sleeping soundly. The man must have truly been worn out from the ordeal of being shot and the following treatment and hospital stay. I was so glad that he was at ease enough at the cottage to fall so peacefully sleep. It made me feel good in a way that I hadn't expected.

Jake shifted a little in his sleep, but then he fell back into the sound pattern of light snores that told me he was truly resting. I didn't mind the sound effects at all. From my position back on the couch, they sounded almost like distant waves crashing against a sandy beach, and I found myself drifting off despite my usual sleep patterns. Maybe, if I was lucky, I'd be able to get in a few more hours myself before it was time to get up and start taking care of Jake again.

I wasn't sure when Officer Grant came and Chief Martin left, but the younger police officer must have stopped off at

Donut Hearts on his way over to the cottage, because I found him eating a donut from the box when I walked outside three hours later.

"Care for one?" he asked me with a grin as he lifted the lid in my direction. "They're good."

"I would expect them to be," I said as I took a lemon-filled from the box. It was delightful, so why was I so disappointed?

"Not as good as yours, mind you, but still good," he added as he wiped his hands.

I looked into the box and counted four donuts left out of a dozen. "You don't have to lie on my account," I said with a grin.

"Hey, the chief took two himself when he left," he said.

"You're kidding. He hardly *ever* eats donuts." In fact, the chief had sworn them off for the longest time after his divorce. He'd lost quite a bit of weight, enough to need new belts and uniforms. Since when had he fallen off of his diet wagon?

"Yeah, well, he seemed to be in a receptive mood when I relieved him," Officer Grant said, "but to be honest with you, it kind of surprised me, too."

"Would you like some coffee to go with the rest of your stash?" I asked as I pointed to the partial glazed donut in his hand.

"Thanks, but I've already had my limit this morning. It took three cups to keep me awake," he said with a slight smile.

"I appreciate you doing this," I said. "You know that, don't you?"

"You're most welcome. I know that the inspector would do the same for me if our roles were reversed, so I'm happy to take a shift."

I realized that was true. Jake was loyal, a good man to have as a friend, but a bad one to have as an enemy. There wasn't much that he wouldn't do for someone he liked, and Officer Grant clearly felt the same way.

"Well, I haven't had my coffee yet," I said as I started inside. "When's Terry coming by to relieve you?"

The young officer seemed surprised that I casually used Officer Hanlan's first name. "By my count, he's due to relieve me in precisely fifty-seven minutes," Officer Grant said as he looked at his watch.

"You can go now, if you'd like. I'm wide awake."

"Thanks, but if you don't mind, I believe that I'll wait until I'm relieved," Officer Grant said. "Oh, by the way, I nearly forgot. Emma and Sharon sent a dozen for you and Jake, too. They're right here under my chair." As he offered them to me, he added, "I've been guarding them as well, free of charge."

I took the donuts from him and smiled. "Would you like me to replace the lemon-filled donut that I took earlier?"

"No, I'm good with what I've got left, but thanks for offering," he said with a grin.

"I'll talk to you later," I said as I headed back in.

"You can count on it."

"Are those donuts?" Jake asked when I walked back inside.

"Freshly made, from what I've been told," I said. "How long have you been up?"

"Not long," he said. "Were you out checking on the troops?"

"Something like that. How did you sleep?"

"Like the dead," he said as he ran a hand through his hair. I noticed that his gaze was still on the boxed dozen donuts still in my hand.

"Would you like one now?" I asked.

"I don't know. I'm not sure that they can live up to your standards," he said with a frown, and I could practically see the drool dripping down his chin.

"There's no sense in being a martyr about it," I said with an easy smile. "I already had one of them myself, and it was delicious."

"Then I'll try to choke three or four down, just to be polite, you know," he said.

I laughed at him as I put the box down and opened the lid. It was chock full of goodness, and it would have taken someone with more willpower than I had to turn any of them down. "Tell you what. I'll grab a plate and a few napkins if you can restrain yourself that long."

"I'll try, but you'd better hurry," he said, smiling.

"Would you like some coffee, too?"

"Yes, please," he said.

I flipped the switch on the coffee pot, then I grabbed two plates and a few napkins before I headed back out into the living room. All in all, I couldn't have been gone more than forty-five seconds.

Jake already had powdered sugar on his chin. He grinned at me as he said, "You were taking so long that I couldn't wait."

I had to laugh right along with him as I found a treat to eat myself. It was a chocolate glazed yeast donut, and it was perfect.

I really wasn't sure how I felt about that, but it didn't stop me from eating all of it anyway.

"You look beat," I told Jake as he came back into the living room after changing into his clothes. We'd eaten, and then he'd decided to change into jeans and a T shirt. While that was my usual attire, Jake was normally somewhat more stylish even when he was off duty, so he looked a little out of place in the clothes he was wearing at the moment.

"It's hard to imagine how much energy it takes me right now just to get dressed," he said as he adjusted his sling. "I hit my arm three times just trying to put my shirt on. I know one thing. I'm going to abandon T shirts and go back to dress shirts until this thing is healed. At least they button up."

"How does your arm feel?"

"I won't lie to you. It hurts getting shot," Jake admitted as he sat heavily down on the couch.

"I would be surprised if it didn't," I said. "You can take another pill for the pain if you'd like to."

"Thanks, but I think I'll give it a little time, first."

I just shook my head and laughed.

Jake asked me, "What's so funny?"

"I already know that you're a tough guy. You don't have to keep proving it to me."

"Actually, I'm trying to prove it to me," he said a little solemnly. "Getting shot has robbed me of some of my confidence quicker than anything I've ever had happen to me before."

I felt bad that I'd laughed. I touched his shoulder as I said, "Jake, you're the toughest man I know. Surely you realize that."

"Suzanne, in all of the years that I've been a cop, I've often wondered what it would feel like to take a bullet." He moved his slinged arm a little, and then he said, "Now that I'm going through it, I'm not quite as brave as I imagined myself to be. It's hard to reconcile who I thought I was with who I really am."

"Don't be so hard on yourself. After all, you're only human," I said.

"Don't remind me," he replied. "Right now it feels as though my arm is going to be this way forever, and I can't stand the thought of being useless."

"Are you okay?" I asked him softly. "I'm worried about you."

"You shouldn't be. I'll be fine," he said. "I guess what it boils down to is that I'm just not all that fond of feeling so helpless, but I'm sure that I'll get used to it sooner or later."

"You're not going to have time to do that," I said. "I know that you're going to be as good as new before you know it."

"I wish that I had your confidence in my healing ability," he said as a hint of a frown began to darken his stern countenance even more. "It sure doesn't feel that way at the moment."

"Hey, nobody said that you didn't deserve a little time to

wallow in self pity, if that's what you really want to do," I said as neutrally as I could.

Jake shot a sharp glance in my direction, held it for a full second, and then he gently nodded. "That's exactly what I'm doing, isn't it?"

"Well, maybe a little bit," I said.

"Or maybe even a lot." He took a deep breath, and then slowly let it out. "There. I'm better now."

"Seriously? That's all that it took?" I asked incredulously.

"Well, that and your company. Suzanne, I know that I'm not the easiest patient in the world, but I'm going to do better from here on out. That bullet missed everything that was vital, and I should be celebrating that fact, not moping around because I can't do everything that I used to be able to do. I'm honestly better now. Thanks."

"I'm not quite sure what I did," I said.

"You called me on my behavior. Isn't that enough?"

"I'd like to think so," I said. "So, what would you like to do now?"

"Do we still have pie?" he asked with a smile, and I knew that I had my Jake back.

"I'll see what I can do," I replied with a grin of my own.

Chapter 11

I heard a car pull up outside a minute later as I was getting Jake his pie. When I peeked out from the kitchen, I realized that Jake must have heard it, too. He started to get up, but I said, "Why don't I check on it myself? You need your rest."

"All I seem to be doing is resting," he protested.

"Good. Then keep up the good work." I looked outside and saw that State Police Officer Terry Hanlan was here. "It's Terry," I said as I headed for the door.

"I'm getting up, Suzanne," Jake said, the resolve clear in his voice. At least he wasn't still feeling sorry for himself. I'd rather have him fighting than giving up any day.

"Do you at least need a hand?" I knew when I'd heard that tone in the past that there was no use arguing, so I might as well try to help.

"No, I can manage just fine on my own, but thanks for the offer." Jake struggled to stand, but to my credit, I didn't make a single move to help him. He was determined to do it on his own, and I wasn't about to take that away from him. He finally found his balance and strength as he stood, but it wasn't without its own drama. I let out a breath I hadn't realized that I'd been holding, but at least he didn't catch it.

As the doorbell rang, my boyfriend answered it himself.

Terry smiled when he saw him, and Jake grinned in return.

"It's good to see you up and about," Terry said as he shook Jake's left hand.

"You know me. It'll take more than a bullet to slow me down," Jake replied. He was doing his best to be cheerful in front of the other state police inspector, something he hadn't tried to do with me. In a way, it made me feel more loved. After all, he had shown me his true feelings earlier, and he hadn't tried to put on a brave face for me. I decided to take that as a compliment.

"That's the spirit," Terry replied. "I hope you don't mind, but I asked Officer Grant to hang around outside while we had a little chat in here."

"No problem," Jake said.

"I'm sure that he's happy to do it," I replied. "He's not just a local cop; he's our friend, too."

Terry looked at me for a moment before he spoke again. "Suzanne, you have every right to refuse my request, but would it be possible for you to step outside with Officer Grant while I have a confidential conversation with Officer Bishop?"

Jake answered before I could. "Terry, you can say anything in front of her that you would say to me alone."

"That's not the way this works, and you know it," Terry said.

"You've got to know that I'm just going to tell her everything that you're about to tell me once you're gone," Jake replied. "We don't have any secrets between us."

"What you do with the information I'm about to convey to you once you receive it is entirely up to you," Terry said firmly. "I hate to be a stickler, but I'm going to have to brief our boss when I get back from vacation, and I'd rather not lie to him, if it's all the same to you."

"Don't say another word. I understand completely," I said as I quickly moved toward the door. "I don't mind going outside."

"Really?" Jake asked me. "Remember, it's your house. You don't have to go anywhere if you don't want to."

"Nonsense. Terry is doing us both a huge favor by taking his vacation time to watch out for us. I'm not about to insult him by demanding that he do something that he's not comfortable with."

"I hate to even ask," Terry said apologetically.

"Don't think another thing about it. Come get me when you're finished."

"Thanks," Jake said. "I really appreciate this."

"I'm happy to do it," I replied as I walked outside.

"What happened? Did they kick you out?" Officer Grant asked me when I joined him outside on the front porch.

"As a matter of fact, I left voluntarily," I said. "It's something about official police business, so I really didn't have any right to be there. Thanks for hanging around so they can chat in peace."

"It's okay. I'm glad to do it. Besides, my shift doesn't start until ten today," he said.

"Still, I'm pretty sure that there are better ways for you to spend your time off than hanging around on my front porch."

"Not with Grace still sleeping," he answered with a smile.

"How's that going?" I asked him.

"Hasn't she said anything to you about us?" he asked, the curiosity thick in his voice. "I just naturally assumed that you knew more about our relationship than I did."

I laughed. "I may have heard a thing or two about it, but if I understand anything, it's that if there are two people involved in something, then there's a good chance that there are at least two ways to describe it. I know Grace's take on things. Now I'm asking you for yours."

"I couldn't be happier, myself," he said with a grin. Though he was holding a conversation with me, it was clear that the brunt of his focus was on the land around us. None of these men ever seemed to stop working.

"Grace seems happy as well," I said.

"Really?" he asked as he studied my expression.

"I wouldn't lie to you. Why do you seem so surprised?"

"Well, we both know that I'm quite a bit younger than she is," Officer Grant admitted. "Sometimes I think she feels odd about being seen out with me. Tell me that it's just in my imagination."

"I wish that I could, but I'm not sure that I can," I answered him as truthfully as I could.

"I see." That seemed to take the wind right out of him.

"Hang on a second. That doesn't mean that this relationship isn't worth pursuing. Grace has had more than her share of trouble with men in the past. Has it ever occurred to you that she might just be looking for an excuse in case this one blows up on her, too?"

"That's not a very promising way to start a new relationship, is it?" He seemed troubled by my comments, and I felt a little bad about being so frank with him.

"Listen carefully to me. I know Grace better than anyone alive, and I think you've got a real chance to make it work, as long as you're in it for the long haul. That's not to say that there won't be some bumps along the way, but anything worth having is worth fighting for, at least in my opinion."

He grinned at me. "Got it. Thanks for the pep talk, Coach."

"I did sound kind of preachy, didn't I?"

"Maybe so, but that's exactly what I needed," he said.

The front door opened, and Terry walked out. Instead of addressing me, he spoke to Officer Grant. "Thanks for sticking around. You can take off now."

"Thank you, sir. I'll be back here at four AM tomorrow."

Terry nodded, and then he handed the local cop his business card. "I want you to know that what you're doing here isn't going unnoticed. If you need anything down the road, and I mean anything at all, I want you to call me."

"Thanks," Officer Grant said as he put the card in his breast pocket, "but I hope you know that's not why I'm doing this."

"I understand that," Terry said with a slight smile. "That's why I gave you my card."

After Officer Grant was gone, Terry said, "He seems like a good man."

"I think so," I said. "Thanks for being nice to him. So, how's Jake doing?"

"He's fine. He wanted me to send you in. Suzanne, I'm sorry about that earlier. You don't know me that well yet, but I'm a stand-up guy. I wouldn't have asked if it weren't important to me."

"There's no need to apologize," I said, and then I added with a grin, "Besides, you heard my boyfriend. He's going to tell me everything that you just told him as soon as I'm inside anyway."

Terry laughed. "You two make a good pair. I'm glad that

he found you."

"Not half as glad as I am," I said. I had a question that I was almost afraid to ask, but I wasn't sure when I might get the opportunity again. "Did you happen to know his wife very well?" Jake's family had died in a car crash quite awhile ago while he'd been on duty, and it had torn out his very soul. It had taken him years to get over his loss and open his heart again to me. I had trouble asking him questions about his wife, but maybe Terry could satisfy my curiosity.

"Yes, I knew her," he said. "She was lovely."

"I've seen her photograph," I said.

"That's not what I meant," Terry explained. "Oh, she was pretty enough, but her beauty came from the inside. She was sweet, kind, and devoted to Jake. It's funny that you'd ask me about her."

"Why is that?" I asked.

"Jake told me not three minutes ago that he'd been lucky in love twice in his life, finding her first, and then you. He loves you, Suzanne."

"That's good, because I love him, too."

"That much is clear." Terry shook his head slightly, and then he added, "You'd better get back in there before he tries to get up from the couch again. He really needs to take it easy."

"Try telling him that. He's struggling right now, but he'll get the hang of it soon enough."

"It wouldn't surprise me one bit," Terry said as he took up the post that Officer Grant had just vacated.

When I walked back in, Jake was staring at the door in frustration. "There you are. I was about ready to send out a search party for you."

"Terry and I had a little chat before I came back in," I said.

"What about?"

"Mostly we talked about how lucky you were to have me in your life," I said with a smile.

"I never denied it," Jake said. "I'm guessing that he didn't talk about Rusk with you, did he?"

"Not a word," I replied. "Have they caught him yet?"

"No, but that's not the worst part of it. The earlier ID in Pennsylvania turned out to be a false alarm. The truth is that we have no idea where he is right now. The FBI is looking for him, but we can't discount the possibility that he's in April Springs. Even with Terry standing guard out front during the day and your friends taking over at night, I don't like just sitting here waiting for him to show up."

"Do we have any choice? You were shot in the arm by his partner, remember?"

"I'm not about to forget that. The thing is, I don't mind being the bait in the trap, but I'm not fond of you being in danger, Suzanne. What if you go stay with your mother and leave me here to face Rusk alone? It will make things a whole lot easier for me if I'm not worried about you."

"How can you be so sure that Rusk is the one who's after one of us? Heather might be out there somewhere trying to get her revenge on me. By deserting you and going to Momma's, I might be putting myself in more danger than if I just stayed here with you."

Jake frowned, and after a moment, he reluctantly replied, "I'll admit that I didn't think about that possibility. You're right. Maybe we should leave things just as they are."

"That sounds like a good plan to me," I said as my cellphone rang. "It's Emma. I hope they haven't had any problems at the donut shop. Do you mind if I take it?"

"Be my guest," he said. "I think I might have another one of her donuts while you two chat. After all, I have to get my strength back up, don't I?"

"Just don't get carried away," I said with a smile. "Hi, Emma. What's up?"

"I might be calling you for nothing, but a state police inspector came by the shop this morning."

"His name didn't happen to be Inspector Terry Hanlan, did it?"

"That's the one. So, you knew that he was in town?"

"As a matter of fact, he's here looking out for Jake," I said. "Thanks for calling, though."

"That's not the real reason that I called. I just wanted to make sure that he was legit," Emma said softly. "Inspector Hanlan brought an artist's sketch by and told me to be on the lookout for some man named Rusk."

"Yes, we think he might be headed this way looking for Jake."

"Well, I might be wrong, but I think he's standing in the donut shop this very second. He asked me where you were, and I had Mom talk to him while I ducked back in the kitchen to call you. You'd better have Jake send someone over here right now, Suzanne. I don't like the way he's looking at my mother."

"Stay on the line. I'm on it," I said as I turned to Jake. "Rusk is in the donut shop!"

"Get Terry!" he barked as he got up off the couch quickly. The movement must have cost him something because I saw him wincing with pain, but it was clear that Jake was ready for action.

"You're not going with him!" I ordered as I flung the door open.

"What is it?" Terry asked, alarmed by my shouting.

"My assistant thinks that Rusk is in the donut shop right now!"

"You stay here!" Terry told Jake as he rushed out the door.

"Jake, you can't go," I said as I stood in his way.

"Get out of my way, Suzanne," he said, almost growling the words at me.

"I won't," I replied, holding my ground and blocking him from leaving. "You're in no condition to tackle a killer."

He thought about trying to get past me anyway, but I watched closely as he finally gave in. Grabbing his cellphone, he dialed a number as I heard Emma on my own line.

"He just ran out the door!" she said, nearly out of breath.

"Should I follow him?"

"*No*!"

"Okay, I just thought I'd ask," Emma said contritely.

"Sorry I yelled, but this man is extremely dangerous. Are you okay?"

"Everyone here is fine," she said. "Listen, I've got to go. That state policeman is back."

She hung up on me, and I debated going to the shop myself, but I knew that my place, at least for the moment, was with Jake. If I went, he'd go with me, and I wasn't at all sure how that would turn out.

"I'm sorry that I had to stop you," I said.

"You did the right thing," Jake said as he tried to hug me. I had to be careful about his arm, but I did my best to hug him back without causing him too much pain. "I got kind of carried away."

"It happens to the best of us," I said as his cellphone rang.

"It's Terry," he told me, and then his face fell. "Rusk got away."

"Then he could be heading this way, and we're not armed," I said, realizing that Rusk's sudden appearance at Donut Hearts may have been a ruse used simply to lure our guard away. It was a short run through the park toward us, and we were wasting precious time. "Where's your gun?"

He reached into his sling and pulled out his service revolver. "It's right here."

"Let me have it," I said as I reached out toward him.

"Suzanne, I'm willing to wager that I'm a better shot left-handed than you are right-handed."

"Maybe you're right," I said as I grabbed my baseball bat. "What should we do now?"

"We lock the door and wait. If he comes for us, we defend ourselves, with deadly force if necessary. Can you do that?"

"To protect us? Just watch me."

"That's my girl," he said with a smile. "Do me a favor. Pull one of the dining room chairs over to the door."

"Are you going to barricade us in?" I asked as I did as he'd requested.

"Nothing quite so dramatic as that," he said as he took the seat. "I just think that I've got a better chance of hitting him if I'm sitting down."

"Then I'll be here as backup," I said. "If you don't take him down, then I will."

"That sounds like a solid plan to me," Jake said, and then we waited.

Chapter 12

By the clock in my living room, it was barely seven minutes between the time Emma had hung up and the present, but it had felt like forever. When at last there was a tap on the door, I pulled my bat back to get ready to swing as Jake called out, "Who is it?"

"Terry Hanlan," he said.

"Go on and get the door, but be careful," Jake said. "He might not be alone."

I opened the door, waiting for something unexpected to happen.

When Terry saw me, he frowned. "I missed him."

"He could still be hiding in the park, couldn't he?" I asked as I pointed behind him.

"The police chief and his men are out there searching right now. I came through the park myself, but I didn't see a sign of anyone there."

After Terry was back inside, I locked the door behind him. It felt really good sliding the deadbolt into place.

"You know, there's something that we have to consider. It might not have actually been Rusk," Jake said after a moment's pause. "You've seen those drawings. They aren't exactly precise, if you know what I mean. I'm willing to bet that his face is generic enough to match a few other men in April Springs, especially if they are strangers."

"That's entirely possible," Inspector Hanlan said, "but thinking that way doesn't get us anywhere. I'm going to call our boss and see if he'll officially put me on guard duty."

"Hang on," Jake said. "We need to talk about this before you do anything that we can't take back."

Inspector Hanlan looked at him oddly. "Jake, we both know that if I make that call, we'll probably have a dozen officers here within the hour patrolling the area."

"And if Rusk sees that, I guarantee you that he's going to run. Is there any doubt in your mind that's going to happen?

If we keep this to ourselves, we still have a chance of catching him."

"Maybe so," he reluctantly said.

"Come on. We both know that it's true," Jake said.

Terry Hanlan leaned forward and stood very close to my boyfriend, who was still sitting down. "Jake, before you and I make any decisions that we might regret later, I want you to ask yourself a couple of things. One, are you comfortable with being the cheese in the trap? And if you are, how do you feel about putting Suzanne in danger, too?"

That wasn't fair. I knew I had to speak up before Jake made up his mind. "Terry, I trust you and Jake and my friends with my life. I couldn't be any safer with a squad of troopers parked on my front porch, and if it means we have a chance to catch this guy on our own, I say we go for it. I'm game for whatever trap you two decide to set."

Jake shook his head. "Suzanne, as much as I'd like to agree with you, I think Terry might be right. Let's get some backup in here right now, and we can worry about Rusk later."

I wasn't about to let it go, though. "Jake, I don't know if you want to keep looking over *your* shoulder for the next thirty years, but I know that I don't want to. If we have a chance to catch Rusk now, then let's not blow it. I say we go for it. I'm betting on us."

Jake grinned at Terry. "I told you she was like this."

"You were right," Terry said.

"So, what do you really think?" Jake asked him. "Be honest with me, Terry. If our roles were reversed, what would you do?"

"It's not fair to ask me that question. There's nobody in my life that I love as much as you love Suzanne." After a moment or two more of consideration, Terry added, "For the record, I'd love to say that she's wrong, but I don't think she is. If we can nab him now, it will be much easier than trying to do it later."

"Then it's agreed," I said. "We're on."

Jake held up one finger. "Not so fast. We'll do it on one condition. If we haven't grabbed him in forty-eight hours, we call in all of the reinforcements we can get."

I nodded in quick agreement. "I can go along with that. After all, if we haven't caught him by then, we probably won't be able to do it at all."

"Suzanne, you have company," Terry said a little later as he knocked on the front door. Jake was in the bedroom taking another nap, so for all intents and purposes, I was all alone.

When I opened the door, I was surprised to find Trish from the Boxcar Grill standing on the porch with a large pot in her hands. "Hey, Suzanne. I didn't realize that I needed a pass to visit you." She was smiling at Terry as she said it, and I wondered what she was thinking when she saw the big state trooper on my doorstep.

"Trish, this is Terry Hanlan. He's a friend of Jake's and mine," I said. It was true, too. While I hadn't known Terry long, he'd been drawn into my circle of friends fast enough. Anybody who was trying to keep me and my boyfriend alive got at least that.

"Nice to meet you, ma'am," Terry said as he nodded briefly.

"Ma'am?" she asked with a smile. "I haven't been called ma'am in quite awhile, and the last man who did it was after a lot more than my soup."

"Sorry, I didn't mean anything by it," Terry said quickly. Was that a blush forming on his cheeks? "I meant it with all respect."

"Well then, we'll just have to see how you act when you're being *disrespectful*," Trish said as she winked at him.

It was time to get Terry off the hook. "Is that for us, or are you just taking your pot for a walk?"

"It's Jake's favorite soup, as a matter of fact, chicken noodle with extra noodles," Trish said with a smile as she handed the pot to me. It was heavy, and clearly full.

"There's enough for everyone, including you," she added as she smiled at Terry. "Should we get you a bowl, too?"

"I'll eat later, but thanks for the offer," he said. "I'd better get back to my post."

After he closed the door, Trish whistled. "Now that is a big hunk of man."

"You're awful," I said with a smile. "I can't believe you made him blush."

"I'm not surprised at all," she said. "After all, that's how I have my fun."

"Did someone say soup?" Jake asked as he came out of the bedroom. "Hi, Trish."

"There he is, the man of the hour," Trish said with a grin when she saw him. "How are you feeling, Jake?"

"Well, right now I'm a little hungry, to be honest with you," he said, looking steadily at the pot. "That smells wonderful."

I hadn't realized that I was hungry as well. "Why don't I dish up four bowls?"

"I'd really like that, but I have to get back to the Boxcar. If you'll fill one for Terry, though, I'll deliver it on my way out."

"What have you been up to with my friend?" Jake asked her with a grin.

"Me? Nothing. Come on, Jake, you know me."

"That's why I asked," Jake said with a grin. "Thanks for thinking of us."

"It's my pleasure. I expect to see you walking across that park soon enough and eating at my place. The exercise will do you good."

"You've got yourself a deal," Jake said.

I set Jake up at the table, and as he started eating, I got a bowl for Terry and filled it up.

"Trish, this is delicious," Jake said.

"It should be. I had one of my girls make it just for you."

I dug out a tray and put a bowl of soup on it, utensils, some crackers, and a soft drink. "Are you sure you don't mind taking this out?" I asked her.

"Honestly, I don't mind at all," she said with a laugh. Turning serious for a moment, Trish said, "Suzanne, if you need anything, and I mean anything, call me. I'm just a footstep away, okay?"

"I will. I promise."

She wouldn't accept it, though. "Suzanne, this isn't a hollow offer. I mean every word of it. You are my dear friend, first and foremost, and I'll do anything that I can for you, up to and including helping you hide a body in the park." She turned to Jake and added, "You didn't hear anything just then, Inspector."

"What? Sorry, I missed that. I was too busy focusing on this delicious soup," Jake said with a smile.

I hugged Trish. "Thanks. I hope that it doesn't come to that, but it's still good having friends like you around."

Trish smiled as she pulled away. "Well, I don't know anyone quite like me, but I appreciate the compliment nonetheless."

After I let her out, I asked Jake, "Should I have gone with her out onto the porch?"

Jake shook his head as he finished another bite. "Don't worry about Terry. He's a big boy. He'll be able to handle her."

"Maybe," I said as I finally got a bowl for myself. I looked at Jake's bowl and asked, "Would you like some more?"

"Maybe just a little," he said. "I'm trying to catch up on all the food I missed while I was in the hospital."

"You don't have to explain yourself to me. I'm just happy to see that you have an appetite."

"I feel like a grizzly bear. All I seem to do is eat and sleep."

"That's all that you need to do," I said as I kissed his head on my way past him.

"Hey, you can eat first before you serve me any more soup."

"This won't take a second," I said as I snatched his bowl so I could fill it up again.

I topped his bowl off and returned it to him, but I didn't get a chance to taste my soup after all.

"More company's here," Terry said.

I left Jake in the kitchen, and I went into the living room. I got there just as Terry opened the door for Hazel, Jennifer, and Elizabeth, the ladies from my book club. Elizabeth held a massive chocolate cake, Jennifer was carrying a lemon meringue pie, while Hazel had a plate of chocolate chip cookies.

"We brought you a few desserts when we heard about what happened," Jennifer said.

"Come on in, ladies," I said as I saw another car pull up. "I'll be right with you," I said as the DeAngelis women from Napoli's Restaurant in Union Square got out.

"We brought food," Angelica, the matriarch, said.

"Enough for two armies," her youngest, Sophia, added.

"They have to eat, don't they?" Angelica asked, and the parade of food began in earnest.

Terry whistled as he saw the food being unloaded. "How many friends do you have, Suzanne?"

"Inspector, I may not have a lot of money, but I'm rich beyond all dreams of avarice when it comes to my friends. Have you ever eaten at Napoli's?"

"No, but Jake's told me about it a few times."

"You're going to want to get a plate when the DeAngelises finish unloading, trust me."

Terry looked mournful. "I'd love to, but I need to stay at my post."

"I'll have Maria bring you a plate," I said.

Terry surveyed the lovely sisters as he asked, "Which one is she?"

"She's the pretty one," I said with a grin.

"You're going to have to narrow it down a little more than that. They're all beautiful, including the mother."

It appeared that Trish was going to have some competition.

As the sun started to fade, the cottage was nearly splitting at the seams with food. That was the way we showed our love in the South, and what I'd told Terry had been true. There was a whole lot of love going on at the moment. I called Momma and Chief Martin to come over and join us, but they had other plans. George was smart, though. He showed up half an hour before his shift to load up a plate, and he'd even brought his secretary, and not-so-secret girlfriend, Polly, with him. Grace put in an appearance, and so did a few other friends as the night wore on. I made up a killer to-go box for Terry before he left, and by the time George was ready to take over his shift, I was afraid that he might be so full that he would fall asleep on duty.

"Are you going to be able to make it until Chief Martin gets here to relieve you?" I asked George as he took over Terry's spot.

"I'm so full I can't nod off," he said. "I should have stopped with my second plate."

"Who can blame you? It's not every day you get that kind of spread laid out for you."

"Don't I know it," he said. "Let me know if you need me. I'll be right outside, wide awake, and that's a promise."

"I trust you, George," I said. "If anybody else comes by, thank them for us, but let them know that Jake needs his rest."

"You've got it."

I closed and locked the door behind me, and Jake and I were in for the night, finally alone.

"Sorry I've been sleeping so much since I got here," Jake said as I added a small log to the fire. It wasn't that chilly, but I liked the ambience of it with its dancing flames and intermittent crackles and pops.

"You don't have anything to apologize for," I said as I settled in next time. "You're recovering from a gunshot wound, remember?"

"I'm not about to forget," he said as he shifted a little,

clearly trying to make himself more comfortable.

"Can I get you anything?" I asked him.

"No, I'm still full from that last plate from the DeAngelis clan. That was really a magnificent spread, wasn't it?"

"I'm glad you liked it, because even with all of the people we fed tonight, there's tons still left over. If we get much more food, we're going to have to use Grace's fridge to store the extras."

"I missed seeing her today," Jake said. "Is everything okay?"

"She came by, but you were resting. Besides, she only stayed for a few minutes. She said that she saw the parade of well-wishers coming up the road to the house, so she decided we might appreciate a little space."

"Thank her for me, would you? That's the nicest thing anyone's done for me today."

He sounded a little grumpy as he said it. "Jake, is everything okay?"

"I hate being the center of attention, Suzanne. You know that."

"I do, but you're going to have to just suffer through it," I said as I mussed his hair a little. "After all, how many folks get the chance to thank a hero?"

"I wish everyone would stop tossing that word around so casually. I was just doing my job. Besides, in all that time I was tracking Monroe, I never knew that Rusk was working with him from the very start."

"Don't be so hard on yourself. No one else knew it, either."

"That's no excuse," he said, and then my boyfriend let out a heavy sigh. "I've been thinking about it a lot ever since I got shot. I'm not sure this is going to work out anymore."

I couldn't believe what I was hearing. Was he actually breaking up with me while I was trying to help him recover from his wound? "You're not tired of me, are you?"

He looked startled by the question. "What kind of thing is that to ask?"

"Based on what you just told me, I think it's a perfectly reasonable question. If you're not getting tired of me, then what is it? Have I done something?"

That's when he must have gotten it. "Suzanne, you and I are just fine. Better than fine, actually. I love you, or do I need to remind you of that more often?"

"It couldn't hurt," I said, feeling better all of a sudden. "If it's not me, then what were you just talking about?"

"The job," he said heavily. "I must be slipping. First I let Morton get a shot off and hit me, and then I find out that I missed learning about Rusk entirely. It's not good."

"You can't hold yourself to such impossible standards, Jake," I said in protest.

"I don't mean to be rude, but I'm the only one who can. When a cop gets stale and burned out, he knows it before anyone else. I've made a couple of pretty big mistakes lately, and it could have cost me more than just some blood and recovery time."

"What are you saying?"

"I'm not sure," Jake said as he stared into the flames. "Not so long ago it didn't seem to matter all that much what happened to me, but now that I've got you in my life, I have a solid reason to live again. Is it worth losing that just for a job?"

"Jake, it's completely understandable for you to second-guess yourself right now, but you're a great cop, and you know it."

"I'm still okay," he said grudgingly. "I'm just not at all sure that I'm as good as I need to be anymore."

"There's one thing I know for sure. You shouldn't try to make any decisions about your future while you're recuperating," I said. "If you still feel this way in a month, then you have every right to entertain the notion of stepping aside, but give yourself a chance to heal first, okay?"

"Are you that dead-set against me retiring?" he asked me softly. There was a hint of hurt in his voice as he asked the question, and I felt a little guilty for not being more supportive.

"Of course not. If it's what you *really* want, then I'll support you a thousand percent. To be honest with you, I'd love to have you puttering around April Springs all of the time."

"You'd still run the donut shop, of course," he said, and he watched me closely as he waited for me to comment.

"I can't imagine doing anything else," I admitted. "I haven't been gone all that long, but I'm still eager to get back to it." As I said it, I realized how it might have sounded to him. "It's nothing against you, Jake. I'm just not sure what I'd do with myself if I suddenly quit making donuts."

"Yeah, I wonder about that, too." Jake yawned, and then he added, "I didn't mean to stir up anything. I just wanted to tell you what was on my mind."

"Please don't ever stop doing that," I said as I kissed his cheek. "I'll be your sounding board anytime."

"But not tonight," he said. "I hate to do this, but I'm going to go crash again. I don't know why I'm so exhausted."

"Well, if it wasn't getting shot, maybe it was being in the hospital. Did they wake you every hour to take your temperature?"

"No, it was always my blood pressure they were worried about," he said with a grin. "What are you going to do if I go to sleep now?"

"Don't worry about me. There's plenty for me to do around here."

"Then I'll say good-night," Jake said, and after pulling himself off the couch, he tottered into Momma's room. I had to stop thinking of it that way, since it was clear that my mother wouldn't be coming back to the cottage to live even after Jake was healed. I was still a bit ambivalent about that fact, but she'd done a noble thing stepping aside so that Jake would have a place to recover, even if she did have motives of her own.

I cleaned a little more, but mostly I just straightened up. I wasn't all that sleepy, even though it was approaching nine o'clock, well past my normal bedtime. The problem was that I wasn't working at Donut Hearts at the moment, the real reason that I was usually able to nod off so quickly. Jake was easy to take care of, that was for sure. When he wasn't sleeping, he was eating or resting on the couch, and none of those activities took a great deal of effort on my behalf. I was wondering if he'd be able to take a month of idleness, but even more pressing a question, could I? Without the shop, I felt a little rudderless, ready to get going, but not exactly sure where, or how.

Finally, I made up the couch again and stretched out with a mystery novel that Momma had left behind. It was about an amateur sleuth who turned to his pet ferret for help in solving crime, an interesting enough premise, I supposed, but it couldn't keep me awake.

Between the fire in the hearth and the tedious prose of the writer, I was asleep before I knew it.

At least I was until three AM the next morning.

When Chief Martin yelled out from the front porch, I came instantly awake, wondering what exactly was going on outside my cottage at that time of night.

Chapter 13

"What's going on?" I asked the chief as I hurried out of the cottage to investigate. I'd stopped long enough to grab my baseball bat, just in case. "Are you okay?"

"I'm fine," he said gruffly as he looked off into the night. Without even glancing back in my direction, he asked, "Did I wake you up?"

"No, not really," I lied. "What happened?"

"I'm not quite sure," he said, his gaze still riveted to the shadows. "I thought I saw something out there, but now I'm not so sure."

"Should I wake Jake up?" I asked.

"No, let him sleep. It was probably just my imagination. This time of night, the shadows can play tricks on your eyes. That must have been what happened." Chief Martin rubbed his hands together. "You wouldn't happen to have any coffee in there, would you?"

"No, but I can make a fresh pot in six minutes."

"Don't go to any trouble on my account," he said.

"It's no trouble at all," I said. "I'll be right back." The air had a bit of a nip to it tonight. "Can I get you a blanket or anything?"

"Thanks for offering, but if I get too comfortable, it might knock me out, and I need to stay alert; thus the coffee," he said with a grin.

"Coming right up, then." I put the baseball bat down beside my chair, close enough to reach if I needed it quickly, but still out of my way.

I walked back in to find Jake awake and standing in the doorway of the master bedroom. "What's going on outside, Suzanne?"

"It turned out to be a false alarm. Chief Martin thought he saw something in the shadows at first, but now he believes it was most likely just his imagination."

"Should I go out there anyway?" Jake asked as he plucked

his revolver off the nearby dresser. He held it a little awkwardly in his left hand, and I wondered if it was all that good of an idea for him to be armed at all.

"There's really no need. Like I said, he's not even sure that he saw something," I said. "I'm making fresh coffee for us. Would you like some, too?"

He yawned before he said, "No, I'd better not. It'll probably just keep me up."

I smiled at him. "I doubt that a brass band and a fireworks display could do that."

"You're probably right, but I still don't want to risk it. Wake me up if anything happens."

"I promise," I said as I headed into the kitchen and turned the coffee pot on. By the time the coffee was ready, I'd cut two slices of apple crumb pie for us, so I filled two mugs and then put everything on a tray. Before I delivered the goods, I stepped into the master bedroom far enough to hear Jake snoring softly. It was truly amazing how much and how easily that man could sleep.

Remembering the cool night, I grabbed a blanket and threw it over my shoulders. Taking the pie and coffee outside, I asked the chief, "Mind if I join you? I've brought some of Momma's apple pie, too."

Chief Martin grinned at me as he took my offerings. "You could have stayed without the bribe, but I appreciate the gesture. I can never get enough of your mother's cooking and baking. Do you have any idea what goes into this topping?" he asked as he took his first bite of pie.

"Have you asked her about it?"

"I've tried, but she won't tell me a thing," he said with a smile. "Come on, spill. I promise that it will be our little secret."

I leaned forward, and then I whispered, "If you promise not to tell anyone else, there's butter, brown sugar, flour, and another secret ingredient in the topping."

"I know about the main items; what I'm after is the secret."

I took a sip of my coffee and then I said with a wry smile,

"I don't know either. She won't even tell me, and I'm her daughter."

"It would be a shame for the world to lose that if something ever happened to her," he said softly. I liked this version of Chief Martin. He was looser, more open at night than he ever was during the day.

"Don't worry," I told him. "She's leaving me a sealed envelope in her will with all of her secrets."

"That's going to have to be one big packet of information," he said without thinking it through.

"I'm telling her that you said that," I teased him.

"Go on. She knows me well enough to realize what I meant by it." There was an easy tone to his response, an assuredness that told me that he and my mother had indeed developed a relationship like one I never thought I'd see her ever enjoy again.

"On second thought, I might just let that one slide," I said as I put my mug down and picked up the plate with my pie on it. "This is amazing, isn't it?"

"Your mother is an amazing woman, so why wouldn't her apple pie be?"

"You don't have to sell *me* on her virtues," I said. As I spoke, I suddenly heard something off in the woods. "What was that?"

"Did you hear it, too?" he asked, putting his pie down and standing up.

"It was probably nothing," I said, trying to dismiss the sound as a normal park noise. I'd done my fair share of camping out in the park growing up, and I knew how noises that sounded so harmless during thc day could be absolutely terrifying once the sun went down.

The world of shadows could be quite a bit more ominous than the one most folks lived with in full daylight.

"I'd still better check it out," he said as he stepped off the porch. "Suzanne, you might want to go inside for a bit."

"I'm staying right here in case you need me," I said as I held my cell phone up. "If you need help, holler."

"What are you going to do with that, phone someone to death?"

I shook my head. "No, this baseball bat is my weapon of choice," I said as I picked it up. "The phone is to call 911 after we clobber the bad guy together."

"I don't mind you grabbing your weapon, but stay here, okay? I'm serious, Suzanne."

"I will," I promise.

Taking a small flashlight from his pocket, the chief pulled out his revolver and lit the way as he walked off into the darkness.

The only thing left for me to do was to wait.

Five minutes later, he was back, and looking a little sheepish.

"Did you see anything out there?" I asked him.

"There's a raccoon over there somewhere," he said as he pointed his flashlight in the general direction of the hanging tree. "He wasn't all that pleased about seeing my light."

"I suppose that sound we heard earlier *might* have been a raccoon," I said.

"Given the circumstances, it's natural enough if we're both jumping at every sound we hear," the chief replied as he sat back in his chair and picked up his coffee.

"Would you like me to warm that up for you?" I offered.

"No, it's just fine the way it is."

"Then I'm off to bed," I said as I grabbed my coffee cup, my empty plate, and most important of all, my baseball bat. "Thanks again for watching over us, Chief."

"Happy to be here," he said.

The only problem was that now I was wide awake, and it had nothing to do with the coffee. I should have been working in the donut shop at the moment, and while my mind knew why I was home, my body wasn't quite so well informed. It was certainly true what they said; old habits were hard to break.

I decided to put the time to good use, so I moved into the kitchen and got out my recipe book. When I'd first opened Donut Hearts, the journal had been my way to constantly strive to come up with new and different things to serve my customers, and it was a habit that I'd grown to enjoy. Flipping it open to a fresh page, I started jotting down notes in my typical random fashion when I was brainstorming with pen and paper.

Make a donut that tastes like a chocolate chip cookie. Better yet, how about those cookies Momma used to make at Christmas, the ones with the peanut butter cookie base and the little dabs of melted chocolate on the top? Speaking of chocolate, how about a hot chocolate donut, with a dollop of marshmallow on top? Marshmallows and bananas might be tasty, or better yet, bananas and chocolate. How about oranges? Okay, the fruit is too runny, but those candy orange slices could be better. I know that I've tried using them before, but I could make them much better than they are now. Could I do a glaze using those? Yum yum. Speaking of candy, remember those little candy hearts we all used to get on Valentine's Day? Could they work in a donut? How about an éclair with rich whipped cream inside, and a topping of crushed candy hearts? How about fillings for yeast donuts? What haven't you tried yet? What goes good with donuts besides milk or coffee? How about a milkshake donut? How would that work? A coffee donut? Maybe a coffee chocolate donut? Why can't I stop thinking about chocolate?

I put my pen down and started rummaging through the kitchen cabinets. Momma liked to keep a little candy stashed away for occasions exactly like this one. No one wanted to make a run to the convenience store in the middle of the night for chocolate. At last, I found an old bag half-filled with Christmas candy tucked behind one of the spare containers of flour. Unwrapping a green foil square, I popped the chocolate into my mouth and bit down. It was still tasty, even though it was most likely past its expiration date, and the next one was even better. After I ate seven pieces, I put the bag back where I'd found it. After all, I was fairly sure that this wouldn't be the last time I got chocolate cravings in the middle of the night.

With my sweet tooth mollified, at least for the moment, I started working again, but this time, before I wrote anything down, I collected an odd assortment of edibles from the kitchen that might conceivably used in donuts or glazes. Powdered sugar was a given for the glaze, as was the cinnamon and the nutmeg. Momma stocked more than just vanilla in her cabinets, though. There were also small bottles of orange and strawberry extract, not to mention containers of cloves, apple and pumpkin pie blends, and even allspice. That certainly might give a donut a distinctive taste. I knew that allspice was used in savory dishes as well as sweet ones, and I wondered how it would go with a sausage and bacon donut. If I could come up with a recipe for that combination, both in the batter and the glaze, I could have a real winner on my hands. Once Jake was fully recovered, I might even let him be my taste-tester for that one.

I decided to play with that idea a little more, but instead of staying in the kitchen, I decided to go back into the living room in case Jake woke up and needed me. It didn't make much sense just sitting there by myself, so I stretched back out onto the couch and threw a light blanket over my legs.

Before I knew what was happening, I was sound asleep, with dreams of flying bacon and singing sausages haunting my dreams.

Jake was still asleep when I checked on him a little just after six AM, and the guard on the front porch had changed again. Officer Grant was out front when I looked out the window, and he grinned as he held up another box of donuts.

I grabbed my blanket again and quietly slipped outside. "Are you stopping by Donut Hearts every morning? They're going to think that you're checking up on them."

"I am, in a way," he said.

"I was just kidding."

"The chief wasn't. Evidently he and Inspector Hanlan had a conversation about the possibility that Rusk might come back, so we're keeping an eye on them, too."

"Not that I'm complaining, but isn't that spreading you all a little thin?"

"Not really," he said. "We're all glad to do it. We're finally back at full staff, so it's not that bad." He reached beside his chair and brought out another box of donuts. "I'm supposed to give these to you."

"What are they trying to do, get me fat?" I asked him.

"I'll take them off your hands if you don't want them," Officer Grant said with a smile.

"If it were just me, I might take you up on your offer, but Jake would kill me if I let those donuts get away. Here, you might as well let me have them now before I change my mind."

Was there a hint of reluctance in his gaze as he gave me the donuts? It couldn't be. After all, he had a smaller box of his own. "Stephen, did you already eat all of your donuts?"

"Hey, I only got three this morning," he said.

"That's more than you ever have of mine," I reminded him.

"Maybe so, but I need something to do here. Nothing's happened since I relieved the chief."

"We heard a raccoon last night. At least that's the theory we decided to go with after the chief investigated," I said.

"That's more than I've heard. I'm wondering if Rusk and Heather have given up and moved on."

"You don't think that they're together, do you?" I asked. It was an unsettling thought having two enemies band together to harm Jake and me.

"No, of course not," he said hurriedly. "I'm just saying, if either one of them has come by, they've seen the guard, and that's just stationed on the outside. For all they know, we could have more folks posted inside."

"Do you think maybe we should?" I hated the idea of having people with guns walking around the rooms of the cottage. While they were positioned outside, I could pretend that it was just me and my boyfriend, but their presence inside would bring the fact home that we both might be in danger all too well.

"No, I don't think it's necessary, unless it would make you feel better," he said.

"Then I think we should leave things just the way they are," I said.

"Good, not that we'd have trouble rounding up volunteers. The chief is getting offers from so many folks that he's having a hard time sorting them all out. In the end, he figured the simpler the arrangements, the better, so we're holding firm with the chief, George, Inspector Hanlan, and me trading off shifts."

"He has a first name, you know. I'm sure that he wouldn't mind if you called him Terry."

"Suzanne, that's not going to happen," Officer Grant said as he took his last bite.

I couldn't resist the sad expression on his face, so I opened my box and offered it to him. "You can have one from here, but just one."

He started to reach in, but then he thought better of it. "No, I'd better not. I'm going to have to do two workouts after work as it is. Thanks, though."

"You're welcome. I'll see you later," I said as I started to go back inside.

That's when I saw a familiar car pull up. What was Grace doing up this time of morning? This was sheer madness.

"What are you doing here so early?" I asked her.

She didn't smile. "I've got a question for you as well. Why is there a woman standing over in those bushes watching you?"

Officer Grant asked, "Grace, is that a joke?"

"If it were, it wouldn't be a very funny one. Go see for yourself. She's standing right over there," Grace said as she pointed toward the road.

"Both of you need to stay here," Officer Grant said

urgently as he headed off to see who might be spying on us.

Grace looked puzzled. "Suzanne, what's going on?"

"Grace, is it possible that you just saw Heather Masterson outside?"

"I thought she was still locked up."

That's when I realized that I'd forgotten to tell her in all the craziness that my life had been experiencing lately. It was a bad mistake, and I was glad that it hadn't proven to be a fatal one. "She was, but she escaped. I'm sorry that I forgot to tell you."

Now Grace looked worried. "Should I have done something about it?"

"What else could you have done, run her over?"

Grace shrugged lightly. "I'm never going to forgive, or forget, that she almost killed my best friend. I believe that a little payback might be in order."

Officer Grant came back a minute later, but he wasn't alone.

Wearing handcuffs and dressed in clothes that obviously didn't belong to her, Heather Masterson was being led up the drive toward us.

"I got her," the police officer said triumphantly.

"You just think you got me," Heather snarled at him as she tried to jerk away.

"That's where you're wrong," he said as he put her in the back of his patrol car.

"I want to talk to you, Suzanne!" Heather yelled out.

"Do yourself a favor and just ignore her," Grace said.

"No, I want to see what she has to say," I answered as I climbed off of the porch and approached the squad car.

"I wouldn't advise you doing this, Suzanne," Officer Grant said solemnly as I neared him.

"I understand, but I'm doing it, anyway," I said. I wasn't reckless enough to get close enough to Heather for her to lunge out at me, though. Stopping three feet away from where she sat, I asked, "Why were you watching the cottage? What were you going to do to me?"

"As a matter of fact, I already did it," she said with a snarl. "You're just too stupid to realize it yet."

"What is that supposed to mean?" The woman was unbalanced; that much was clear.

"You're the one who's supposed to be so clever. You figure it out," Heather said, and then she tried to spit on me. "How's your boyfriend doing?" she asked with a wicked grin.

My thoughts went immediately to Jake, alone inside the house.

As I ran for the front door, I screamed at Heather, "If you hurt him in any way, I promise you that I'll come back and kill you."

Chapter 14

Jake must have woken up from my scream. As I burst into the cottage, he called out from the master bedroom, "What's going on out there?"

"Officer Grant just caught Heather Masterson, along with a little help from Grace," I said as I tried to catch my breath. "Jake, are you okay?"

"Well, I'm a little hungry, but other than that, I'm fine," he said as he came out of the bedroom. "Are there any donuts left?"

I had to laugh. "I've got a fresh batch outside. I'll bring them right in."

"Hang on. I'm coming outside with you." He stood a little firmer this time, but slipping the robe over his shoulders was too much. "Suzanne, give me a hand, would you?"

"Is he all right?" Grace asked as she burst into the cottage before we could leave.

"I'm fine," Jake said lightly. "Why is everybody so worried about me all of a sudden?"

"Heather acted as though she hurt you," I explained.

"Thank goodness she was lying," Grace said. "I'll go tell Stephen that everything is fine here, and then I have to get to work."

"We'll go out with you," Jake said. "I want to see Heather for myself."

We all walked outside together, and though the back door of the cruiser was now firmly closed, it was easy to see that Heather was fuming as she sat inside.

"We got her, sir," Officer Grant said proudly.

"Well done," Jake replied. "Did she say anything to you after you caught her?"

"She's been rambling a little, but the woman is clearly off, so I wouldn't pay any attention to anything that she says," Officer Grant said.

"She still might have useful information for us," Jake said.

I volunteered, "Like I said before, she implied that she'd already hurt you when Officer Grant caught her. It might have been an empty threat, but it still scared the life out of me."

"She didn't do a thing to me, Suzanne," he said.

"I know that, now."

At that moment, the police chief himself drove up, his lights flashing and his siren wailing. As he popped out of his car, he asked, "What's the status here?"

"The escaped prisoner is safe and secure in the back of my cruiser," Officer Grant reported.

"Good work. Take her to the jail, and I'll join you there shortly."

Officer Grant nodded, and as he drove off with Heather, he saluted me.

I knew there was still one threat still out there, but having Heather back in custody allowed me to breathe a little easier.

"Well, that was a little more excitement than I expected this morning," Jake said as we went back into the cottage. "I can't believe Heather came after you like that."

"I have a hunch that she came looking for us," I said. "I'm just glad somebody stopped her before she could do anything to harm either one of us."

"Did she happen to have a weapon on her?" Jake asked me.

"Not that I heard. Why?"

Jake frowned for a moment before he answered me. "She wasn't going to strangle us, Suzanne. If the woman *was* going to try to hurt us, she would have had to have something on her. It's too hard to believe that she planned to break in here and find something to use against us. I need to talk to Chief Martin."

"Mind if I tag along?"

"Are you kidding? I'm counting on it," Jake said as he opened the front door. The chief was on the phone, and he looked startled to see us rejoining him so soon.

In a near-whisper, he concluded his telephone conversation

by saying, "I thought you'd like to know. I'll tell her. Okay, I'll tell them both. Love you." After he put his phone away, he said a little sheepishly, "That was your mother."

"I certainly hope so," I said. "Were you bringing her up to date on what happened?"

"She wanted me to keep her posted," he said. "I hope you don't mind."

"Hey, I should be thanking you. After all, you saved me a phone call," I replied.

"I thought you two were going to stay inside?" the chief asked. "Don't worry about a guard. I'm staying put until Terry gets here."

At least someone was treating the state police inspector as an equal by using his first name.

Jake spoke up and asked his question. "Did Heather have any kind of weapon on her when Officer Grant arrested her?"

The chief frowned. "No, he told me that she was clean."

"Then what was she doing here?" Jake asked. "We need to investigate the area where Heather was hiding. I'd feel a lot better if we found something she discarded when she was discovered."

"That's a good point," the chief said.

"Grace saw her over there," I said as I motioned to some bushes close to the road.

"Then let's walk over there and have a look around," Jake said.

"Are you up to doing that?" I asked him.

"Suzanne, I appreciate your concern, but I'm tired of just sleeping and eating." He paused, and then added, "Well, I'm not done with either one of them quite yet, but I do need to start moving around some again."

"I get that," I said.

"I bet you're ready to get back to work already yourself, aren't you?" my boyfriend asked me with a grin.

"I'm fine," I said, completely skirting the question. "If you're up to it, let's go, but we don't have to rush. If you need to go at your own pace, we're both fine with that, right,

Chief?"

"Absolutely," Chief Martin replied. "We've got all of the time in the world."

When the three of us got to the bushes, it was clear from the crumpled low-lying brush that Heather had been standing there for some time. I found a few pieces of wrapped candy in the grass that looked as though they'd fallen out of her pockets, so she'd obviously made herself right at home. Chief Martin tucked them into an evidence bag as I asked Jake, "What exactly are we looking for?"

"Anything that might be used as a conventional weapon," Jake said.

We started searching the immediate area, but there was nothing there out of the ordinary. When the three of us met up in the road again, Jake was frowning. "That's odd."

"It does beg the question why she was here," the chief said.

"Maybe she wasn't intent on hurting us after all," I suggested. "She could have just been spying on us."

Jake shook his head. "That's not her style though, is it? She poisoned her aunt and she threatened you with a knife. This isn't a woman who just watches things to see what happens."

"I don't know," I said. "Maybe being locked up changed her."

"That could be it," Jake reluctantly admitted. "Who knows? Maybe she planned to use one of your kitchen knives on us once she got inside."

"Then I'm glad that we had a guard posted out front, and I'm even happier that Grace happened to drive up at the perfect time," I said.

"So am I," the chief said.

We were all back on the porch when Officer Hanlan drove up. "It appears that I missed all of the excitement this morning," he said as he approached us.

"How did you hear about it so quickly?" I asked him.

He grinned. "I keep my police band radio tuned into the local channels so I can keep up with what's going on in the area I'm working."

"But you're not working right now," Jake said with a grin. "You are on the oddest vacation that I've heard of, but you're not on the clock."

"Like you wouldn't do the same thing for me," Terry said to him warmly.

"Probably."

"Definitely," Terry said, and then he turned to me. "Suzanne, are you okay?"

"I'm fine," I said.

"That's good." The state inspector turned to the police chief. "I'm here to relieve you. I'm sure you've got a prisoner you'd like to interview. If you don't mind, I'd like a word with her myself later, if we could arrange a substitute sentry."

"That would be fine," Chief Martin said. "What did you want to talk to her about?"

"I'd like to know what she was doing here, and how she planned to hurt these folks," Terry told him. "I gather from what I heard over the radio that she wasn't armed. Have you searched the area for a weapon?"

"Great minds think alike," Jake said with a grin. "We just checked the vicinity. There was nothing there."

"Not unless you count a few pieces of candy," I said with a laugh. I'd never seen Jake interact with a peer, and it was enlightening. "Would you guys like some coffee? I'm about to brew a fresh pot for myself, but I might be persuaded to share."

"That sounds great, but I have to be on my way," the police chief said reluctantly.

"How about you, Jake? Keep me company while Suzanne's busy inside?" Terry asked.

"Sounds good," he said.

"Don't worry," Terry told me. "I won't keep him long. I'd hate for him to miss his morning nap."

"I think I'm pretty well rested at the moment, but thanks for thinking of me," Jake answered with a sarcastic smile.

As Chief Martin drove off, I left the two men on the porch together. It would be great for Jake to have that interaction, and the more I thought about it, it was something that I could use as well. After I made the coffee, I had an idea of what to do next, if Jake was game for it.

The coffee made, I put three mugs on the tray and added the box of donuts Officer Grant had brought earlier. The two men were deep in conversation as I walked out, but it stopped abruptly when they realized that I was there. "Don't stop chatting on my account," I said as I handed out the mugs.

"Don't mind us. We're just brainstorming," Jake said.

"About what, exactly?"

"How to flush Rusk out," Terry said. "We both realize that if we don't do something soon, our boss is going to swoop in here and run him off for good, and that's not going to help any of us sleep better at night."

"Have you come up with anything yet?"

"Not so far, but we're working on it," Jake said. When he spotted the Donut Hearts box, he asked me, "Donuts for breakfast again?"

"Are you actually complaining about that?" I asked him with a smile.

"No. It's not that. They're good, but they can't hold a candle to the ones that you make," he said. How did he manage to feign reluctance as he picked up a lemon-filled donut?

"You don't have to eat it, you know," I answered with a hint of laughter in my voice.

"I don't want to offend Emma and her mother," Jake said, and then he took a large bite.

"I'd hate to do that myself," Terry said as he grabbed one for himself.

"Should I leave you two alone so you can get on with your planning session?" I asked. "I don't mind. All you have to do is ask."

"Thanks, but we both need to mull over this before we talk

again," Jake said.

After we ate, sharing a little pleasant conversation that didn't involve crazed murderers, Jake said, "That was good, but I'm getting a little restless. Suzanne, how would you feel about taking a little walk in the park?"

"Funny, I was just going to suggest it myself," I said. "Jake, are you sure that you're up to it?"

"If I'm not, there are plenty of benches where I can rest that are scattered all over the place, so I think I'll be fine."

"You don't mind if I tail you both, do you?" Terry asked.

"We're perfectly safe in the park," Jake replied.

"You probably are, but I'm not going to have Rusk take a run at you on my watch." There was a new air to the state police inspector's tone, one that didn't allow any room for debate. I'd heard it in Jake's voice a few times in the past myself, and it amazed me that Terry had it as well.

"What about the cottage?" I asked.

"He won't mess with it if you're both out," Terry said. "Just to be sure, though, I'll sweep it myself when we get back. No worries on that account."

"Jake, is that okay with you?" I asked.

My boyfriend shrugged his shoulders as he said, "It seems that I don't have any choice in the matter." Before Terry could reply, Jake turned to him and said, "You know how it is. I appreciate your point of view, and of course, you're right. I know it in my heart, but I'm just not crazy about admitting it. Right now, I'm well aware of the fact that I couldn't bring down a teenage girl shoplifting lipstick in a department store."

"Don't sweat it, my friend. You'll be back before you know it," Terry said, putting a kindly hand on Jake's good arm.

"You bet I will." Forcing himself to smile, Jake turned to me and asked, "Now, who's ready to take a walk?"

"I am," I said happily. It would be good for both of us to get outside for a little exercise and fresh air. "While we're out, we can stop by Donut Hearts and see how they're doing."

"Please, just no more donuts," Jake said overdramatically.

"Don't worry. You're safe. I just want to chat with Emma and Sharon," I admitted.

"So, there's an ulterior motive to this walk, is that it?"

"No, the main motive is to get you moving," I told him. "Me being able to pop into my donut shop will just be a happy bonus. Besides, you two don't have to go inside. You can sit out front and get back to making your grand plans."

"In that case, I'm on board one hundred percent," Jake said with a grin. "Let's go."

It was a beautiful morning to take a walk in the park, with the sun warming the day nicely as we strolled around at a leisurely pace. Terry was kind enough to give us some space, and for a brief time, I nearly forgot that he was even there. We only had to stop twice to rest on our brief walk to the donut shop, and I was proud of Jake for doing so well so soon after going through such a traumatic experience.

"Hey, you did great," I said when we got there as he collapsed onto one of the chairs I kept out front for folks who liked to dine on their donuts al fresco.

"I guess so," he said, a little out of breath. "You wouldn't happen to have any water in there, would you?"

"I'll go grab you a bottle," I said as Terry joined us. "Would you like anything from inside?"

"No thanks. I'm good," he said as he glided down onto the chair beside Jake.

"Showoff," Jake said with a hint of a grin. It was clear that he was pleased with his progress, no matter how much he might complain about it.

"You'll be back in the saddle in no time," Terry said. "Don't worry; you'll get your wind back soon if you can keep up that pace."

"I'd better."

"And so the prodigal returns," Emma said with a smile as I

walked into Donut Hearts. It felt odd being on the wrong side of the counter while the store was open.

"I need to grab a water for Jake, and then I'll be right back," I said as I took a bottled water from the open fridge beside the counter. "Put this on my tab."

"You got it, boss," she said. Emma and I kept tabs on what we took from the shop, more because of inventory control than actually collecting money. I liked things to add up, especially when we ran our totals at the end of every month.

"Here you go," I said as I gave Jake the water.

He barely noticed me as he took it from me. "Thanks."

"I'll be back soon," I told the men.

Jake nodded absently as he said, "Take your time," and Terry didn't even manage that.

I had a hunch that I would have been able to finish the shift inside without either one of them ever noticing my absence. These two men had remarkable powers of concentration when they were working on a problem. I didn't even feel bad about my motive to get Jake out and walking.

It had done what I'd hoped, and now I had a chance to see how my donut shop was really doing. Maybe, for just a few minutes, I'd get back that sense of normalcy that I'd been missing over the past few days.

Chapter 15

"I'm back," I said as I walked inside Donut Hearts again. "Did you miss me?"

"More than I can ever express," Emma said with a grin. I knew that working the front wasn't her favorite job to do at the donut shop, and I was a little surprised to find that her mother wasn't running the counter instead.

"Where's your mom?" I asked as I looked around at the nearly spotless front area.

"At the moment, she's up to her elbows in dirty dishes, gaining a new appreciation for what I do more and more by the hour," Emma answered.

"You're not making her do *all* of the dirty bowls, trays, cups and dishes, are you?"

"No, I helped her out a little before we opened, and I'm lending a hand at the end of the day, too. She's not nearly as fast at it as I am."

"That's because you've had lots and lots of practice," I said.

She smiled. "You bet I have. I've got to say, I have a new respect for you as well, Suzanne. Running this place without you even for a few days has really taught me a lot."

"How so?"

"My question for you is: How do you manage to do this every day without going crazy?" she asked me. "It's absolutely exhausting."

"You should know. You're here with me six days a week," I reminded her.

"Sure, but that's just as your assistant," Emma said. "It's a whole different ballgame being the one in charge. I've got to say, I'm truly impressed."

"Don't worry. You'll get the hang of it soon enough," I assured her.

"I hope you're right." Emma leaned closer and lowered her voice as she added, "I can't believe they caught Heather spying on you this morning. Wild, huh?"

"It was wild, all right. If Grace hadn't come along, I'm not sure we would have ever caught her. In a way, it's kind of crazy the way it worked out."

"As long as she's back in jail, that's all that matters," Emma said. "Dad's planning to run the story this afternoon in a special edition of the paper. He's planning to drag up the old case, and he's even including Heather's mug shot with the story." Emma's father and Sharon's husband, Ray, ran the town newspaper, and he never could pass up a good story. He'd even run a piece on Jake's heroics the day before, but I'd kept it from my boyfriend. I was certain that Jake wouldn't approve of the glowing praise in the article, nor the photograph Ray had chosen to use. Where he'd managed to find Jake's photo from his police academy graduation was beyond me. Even I had trouble recognizing my boyfriend from the grainy photo.

"How's Jake doing, by the way?" Emma asked.

"I'm encouraged by how quickly he's healing, to tell you the truth. He even walked over here with me from the cottage."

"He's here?" Emma asked as she looked around outside.

"Yes, but he probably won't come in this time. He's outside with his guardian angel, as a matter of fact," I said as I explained Terry Hanlan's presence to her.

"Inspector Hanlan sounds like a good friend to have," Emma said.

"He is at that," I answered as the front door opened. I half-expected to see Jake or Terry come in, but it was my ex, Max, instead.

"I just said hi to Jake," Max said as he approached. "So, you're back making donuts already, are you? That break didn't last very long, did it?"

"I'm not working, Max. I'm just here visiting."

"It must be killing you standing on the sidelines," he said good-naturedly.

"Not as much as you might think," I answered. "How's

Emily doing?" Max and Emily Hargraves had been engaged recently, but unlike Max and me earlier, they hadn't made it all the way to the altar, though they were still dating.

"She's absolutely perfect," Max said with a sincere grin. Honestly, I never thought I'd be able to say it, but I was happy that my ex-husband had found his one true love at last. "As a matter of fact, that's the real reason that I'm here." He turned to Emma and said, "Emily's craving a chocolate éclair again. Please tell me that you have at least one left."

"I happen to have two," Emma said happily.

"Even better. I'll take them both."

As Emma boxed the treats up, I said, "I haven't been by her shop lately. How are the guys dressed at the moment?" The guys I was referring to were Emily's shop's namesakes, Two Cows and A Moose, named in honor of her childhood stuffed animals that still played prominent roles in her life. She had dressed them in some outlandish garb in the past, and it had turned out to be a real drawing power for her store.

"That's a funny story. We had just watched an old movie of Robin Hood, so she has them dressed in felt outfits, hats included. I made them all tiny bows and quivers filled with real little arrows in keeping with the general theme. If I say so myself, they look great."

"I'll have to get by and see them before she changes them again. Is she still keeping that scrapbook with pictures of all of their outfits?"

"It's the only way she can keep track of everything," he said. It was clear that Max had fully bought into the premise that Cow, Spots, and Moose were just as real as anyone else, something that I knew Emily loved him for. In the end, it seemed that the two of them were a great match, despite my earlier misgivings about the pairing.

"Have you two had a chance to reschedule that wedding of yours?" I asked.

Max shrugged. "We're in no hurry, but when we do, you'll be one of the first ones to know. After all, we wouldn't be together if it weren't for you."

"Don't give me too much credit," I protested.

"You shouldn't be so modest, Suzanne. You did me the biggest favor anyone has ever done for me in my life the day you talked Emily into giving me another chance." He lightly kissed me on the cheek, paid for the éclairs, grabbed the box, and then took off.

"I still can't get over how well the two of you get along these days," Emma said.

"Hey, people can change."

"I know that they can, but it doesn't feel like they do all that often."

"Then that's even more reason to celebrate it when it does happen," I said. "How has business been over the past few days?"

Emma frowned a little as she said, "It's good, though I've had a few complaints that my donuts aren't as good as the ones you make. I don't see how that's possible, since I'm using the same recipes that you use, but it's true. I taste samples every now and then of the ones that Mom and I create, but they don't have that little something extra that yours seem to."

I had to laugh. It felt good that I was still needed after all. Since I'd handed over the reins of the store to Emma and her mother, I'd been feeling as though they'd picked up where I'd left off without skipping a beat, and for some reason, that fact had saddened me. "Try not to take it too personally, Emma. You know that I get complaints all of the time, too, so do your best not to let it bother you."

"It's kind of hard not to, though, isn't it? Working in the front of the store is kind of like being on the Internet. People can be really mean, can't they?"

I had to laugh at her analogy. "I don't know; I find some folks on the Web can be much meaner than the ones I run into in real life, and some of those folks have been killers."

"It's a cold and cruel world out there all around, isn't it?" Emma asked.

"It can be, but there are a lot of good things in it, too.

Don't ever forget that."

"I won't be able to, not as long as you're around," Emma said. "You're not going anywhere anytime soon, are you?"

"I hadn't planned to," I said. "You don't mind me just popping in like this, do you?"

My assistant laughed. "Are you kidding me? I thought you'd be here yesterday. Donut Hearts will always be your place, Suzanne, no matter how long you're gone. Come around as often as you'd like. Oh, no."

I wondered about the last part of her statement. "Pardon me?"

"It's not you," she said as she pointed over my shoulder. "Two vans from the Senior Center just pulled up. I didn't know they were coming."

I knew those guys and gals could be a real handful from firsthand experience. "Would you like me to stick around and lend a hand?"

"No thanks. It's too late for me, but save yourself," Emma replied with a smile.

"I'll leave you to it, then," I said as I walked out the door, stopping to hold it for the streaming band of eager treat-lovers making their way inside.

"Are you two ready to go?" I asked as I approached Jake and Terry.

"Are you finished already?" Jake asked me, clearly surprised that I was ready to go. Was there a hint of disappointment in his voice as he'd said it?

"Why, would you like me to go back in and give you two more time?"

"It's not that," Jake said. "I was just hoping for a little longer time to rest up for the trek back."

"Tell you what I'll do," I said. "Why don't I go back and grab my Jeep while you two stay here? I can come back and get you both so neither one of you have to walk."

"I'd rather you didn't do that," Terry said gravely.

I saw Jake shake his head subtly, trying to warn his friend off the approach he was about to take with me, but his coworker failed to read the sign.

"Sorry," I said lightly.

"Does that mean that you won't do it?" Terry asked.

"No, it just means that I'm sorry that I have to disappoint you," I answered with a pleasant smile.

"Suzanne, you could be in significant danger if you go back to the cottage alone," Terry said, and then he turned to his friend. "Jake, help me out here."

"I'm just an innocent bystander here. You're on your own, pal," Jake said.

I touched Terry's hand lightly. "Listen, I appreciate the gesture, but Jake needs a ride, and I'm going to provide it. They caught my stalker this morning, remember?"

"You know what? I'm feeling better all of a sudden. I could probably walk now," Jake said as he started to get up.

"Nonsense," I answered as I put my hand on his good shoulder. I was chafing a little at all of the attention I'd been getting lately, and while I was willing to put up with it from Jake, I needed a little space for myself. "You're not going anywhere, mister."

Jake nodded, accepting that this was about way more than walking now.

"I can go with you myself," Terry said reluctantly as he started to stand.

"If you do that, then who's going to watch Jake? Isn't he the most important target here?"

"You're more important than I am," Jake said.

I touched his cheek lightly. "I appreciate you saying that, but you need to tell your friend here that I'm going to go get my car, alone, and that I'll be back soon."

"Is she always this stubborn?" Terry asked Jake in clear frustration.

"Only when it's important to her that she gets her way. You might as well give it up, Terry. You're not going to win this one."

The state police inspector struggled a few more seconds, and then he finally nodded. "I'll agree to this on one condition. You need to be available to me on the phone the entire time in case there is trouble, so don't call your mother or your best friend while you're walking to your Jeep. Will you at least agree to that?"

I didn't like it, but I could see that he had a good point. "Fine."

"Very good," Terry said, and then he asked me, "Why do I feel as though we both just lost this argument?"

"Keep telling yourself that if it helps you sleep at night," I said, and then I kissed Jake lightly on the forehead. "I'll be right back, so don't you go anywhere."

"Where would I go?" he asked with a smile before he added softly, "Don't take any crazy chances, okay? Just get the Jeep and come straight back here. Stay out of the house; will you do that for me?"

"I will, but just for you," I agreed.

I decided to take advantage of the situation and get out of there before either man could change their mind. I knew that Terry, and to a lesser extent Jake, were both just watching out for me, but I was a grown woman, and I couldn't take being under constant supervision and surveillance.

Even though it was a short walk back to the cottage, I relished the idea of being out on my own.

I just hoped that there was no reason for any of us to regret my decision to go alone.

Chapter 16

As I walked down the road to my place alone, I began to regret my decision to ignore Terry's advice. With every step, I could feel the gazes of a multitude of bad men peering out at me, daring me to take one step into the park that I knew so well. I had the creepiest feeling in my gut that if I veered off course even a single step, something dark and evil would swallow me whole. Even though it was broad daylight, I still couldn't shake the feeling, but honestly, if it had been dark out, I never would have insisted that I go alone. Today, there was no comfort in the light, though.

The short walk seemed to take forever, but I finally turned the last corner and saw my Jeep sitting there in the driveway.

But that still didn't mean that I was safe. The plastic windows weren't exactly secure, and I knew anyone with the least amount of determination could get inside. Hadn't Max sneaked in once when he'd been hiding from the police? How hard would it be for Rusk to slip inside and wait for me in the backseat, ready to choke me the second I got in?

I circled the Jeep twice before I was confident that it was safe to get in and drive away. After I was as sure as I could be, I jumped inside and slammed the flimsy door behind me. Jamming the key into the ignition, I prayed for the engine to start and get me out of there before anything bad could happen.

Only the blasted thing wouldn't start.

I'd flooded the engine in my haste to get out of there, and so I had to wait the longest two minutes of my life before I tried to start the engine again. I'd learned long ago that the two-minute break was required for this particular vehicle, and I was usually a little more careful about pumping the gas before I tried to start it, but what could I say? I'd panicked, and now I was paying for my rash behavior.

The entire time I waited, my gaze kept darting all around me, front to back, side to side, but always on the lookout for someone evil coming for me.

I finally couldn't take it any longer. I tried starting the engine again, and this time the Jeep sprang to life. Shoving it into gear as I took the emergency brake off, I sped back to the donut shop, only to find Jake and Terry walking down the road toward me.

After I stopped in the middle of the road, I opened my window and asked them, "Why didn't you two wait? That was the plan, remember?"

"What took you so long?" Jake asked, the relief obvious on his face. "We thought something might have happened to you."

"I flooded the engine," I admitted. "Sorry about that. I didn't mean to scare you both."

"It's fine now," they said as Terry climbed into the back and Jake sat beside me. I turned the Jeep around and then I drove us back to the cottage in short order. With the company of two state police inspectors, the woods lost a lot of their earlier menace in my eyes.

"Did you see anything along the way?" Terry asked me as we approached the cottage.

"Nothing but monsters hiding in every shadow," I said. "I admit it. I was nervous."

"Not half as frightened as we were for your safety," Jake said.

When I got to the cottage, Terry said, "Let me out, Jake, but then I want you to get back into the Jeep. Suzanne, be ready to take off the second you hear or see anything out of the ordinary."

"We're not leaving you if something goes wrong in there, and you can't make us," I said, and Jake nodded his approval.

It was clear that Terry wanted to argue with us, but in the end, he just smiled as he shook his head. "Suit yourself, but if somebody kills all three of us, don't blame me."

After three long minutes, I asked Jake, "Should we go check on him? He's been in there an awfully long time."

"No worries, Suzanne. Terry's just being thorough," my boyfriend said, but it was clear that he was a little unsure himself.

"Maybe so, but I'm giving him one more minute, and then I'm calling Chief Martin," I replied firmly.

"I wouldn't do that if I were you," Jake said.

"Why not?"

"If something has happened to Terry, I'm not sure the Chief will be able to help him. If it comes to that, I'll go in myself."

"With a bad arm? What are you going to be able to do to help him?" I asked him.

"I'm not sure, but I have to try," Jake said. "It's the only way I'd ever be able to live with myself if something happened to him while he was guarding us."

Now I spent the last seconds hoping beyond hope that Jake wouldn't have to go inside as backup. If Terry, just as well trained as my boyfriend and healthy to boot, couldn't stop Rusk, what chance did Jake have? He didn't even have the use of his right arm. I decided that no matter how much Jake protested, I was going to go into the cottage with him. Between the two of us, we might just be able to stop Rusk. I was sure that Jake would fight me on my decision, but he really wasn't going to have any choice. If he'd thought that I was being stubborn before, he was about to be in for a real glimpse of how hard I could dig in my heels when I needed to.

"That's it. Time's up," Jake said as he opened the passenger door of the Jeep.

I opened mine as well. "Then I'm going in with you."

"You most certainly are not," he said in that commanding voice of his. I was sure that it worked just fine on criminals and even coworkers, but it didn't have any sway with me.

"Just try and stop me," I said as we both stood in the driveway.

We didn't have to argue anymore, though.

Terry stepped out of the cottage with a relaxed smile on his face. "It's all clear inside," he said. "What are you two doing standing outside of the vehicle? I thought I told you both to stay in the car."

"Apparently *nobody's* following orders today," Jake said.

"You can pout all you want to," I told him, "but I'm not about to stand idly around while you two put yourself in danger for my sake."

"That's what we've been trained to do, though," Jake said.

"I know that, but it doesn't mean that I'm not every bit as brave as you two are."

"Make her understand what I'm trying to say, Terry," Jake said to his friend.

"You're kidding, right? Honestly, I'd rather face Rusk alone barehanded than get into the middle of this," he said with a grin. "Hey, is anybody else hungry?" he asked, clearly trying to diffuse the tension of our conversation.

"It *has* been awhile since we ate those donuts," Jake said, letting the darkness of our discussion slip quickly away. "I wonder if there's any food from Napoli's left in the fridge."

I had to laugh. "There's at least a week's worth of goodies from Angelica alone." The two state police inspectors had dropped our previous arguments completely, and I really had no choice but to follow suit. It was a good thing, too. I wasn't about to change my mind. From now on, if they were going to put their lives on the line, then I was going to do it with them. What I lacked in training, I would more than make up for with sheer determination.

While the men stayed out on the porch keeping guard, I went in and started reheating leftovers. Everything had been so delicious that it was hard to decide which meal to serve, so instead, I heated pans of lasagna, ravioli, and spaghetti with meatballs. As I prepped the plates on the tray that had been getting a great deal of use lately, I reached for a caramel candy in the bowl on the counter. Momma was constantly picking up new treats to nibble on, and I had to wonder how she managed to stay so petite, whereas if I even looked at a piece of candy, I seemed to find a way to gain weight. It wasn't until I started to unwrap the caramel in my hands that I remembered it had been Heather's candy of choice. I'd even found some in the bushes where she'd been watching us. I knew that it wasn't the candy's fault, but I couldn't bring myself to eat a single piece of it, its association with the killer so close in my mind. With a shudder, I returned the candy to the bowl and pushed it all away; oddly, it somehow made me feel a little better, and that was something that I was determined to embrace. As I looked around the kitchen, I knew that this cottage was more than just a place to sleep at night. It meant home to me, and the thought that I had to have an armed guard present out front in order to live there made me sad. That wasn't the only reason for my melancholy, though. Momma had lived there my entire life, and now, in part directly because of me, she was gone. I knew what she'd said about starting a new life away from our cottage, and I understood her rationale, but that still didn't make it any easier living there without her now. I knew that it would have sounded crazy if I'd told anyone else what I was feeling, but even though two men were just steps away out on the front porch, I was lonely. There was something that I could do about that, though.

Fortunately, she picked up on the first ring. "Suzanne, is everything all right there?" she asked after I identified myself.

"Everything's fine, Momma."

"That's wonderful news. I didn't want to smother you, but I've been hoping you'd call," she said.

"I know how this must sound, but I miss you." It took all that I had not to break down over the phone. I tried to give myself a pep talk about keeping a stiff upper lip, but it didn't work.

"I miss you, too," she said, and then she laughed with relief. "What a fine pair of fools the two of us make."

"Does it really matter if nobody else understands us?" I asked her.

"Not in my mind. You must be relieved that Officer Grant caught Heather."

"It's a load of my mind, but there's still one bad guy out there gunning for us," I reminded her.

"Yes, and this Rusk sounds like a very wicked man."

"He does indeed," I said. "I didn't call to talk about him, though. How are you settling into your new place?"

"It's not as easy as I'd hoped it would be, to be honest with you," she said.

"You can always move back here with us, you know," I suggested, only halfway kidding.

"No, that wouldn't be too awkward at all, would it?" she asked as she laughed a little. "Just the three of us, all living cozily under one roof."

I laughed some myself at the thought of it. "You know, we can always make Jake move out. At the rate he's going, he's not going to need me in another week, anyway. I've got to tell you, he's tougher than I even thought he was."

"He would have to be, wouldn't he? Thank you for your gracious offer, but I honestly believe that the only way I'm going to be able to move on with my life is to leave the cottage behind. We both know that there are a great many reasons that a fresh start is called for right now."

"Does that mean that I should move out, too?"

"Of course not; it suits you. Besides, you never lived there when you were married to another man. That's a big difference between the two of us."

"I can see that," I said, but before I could speak again, the oven timer went off.

"What are you cooking?" Momma asked curiously. While I was adequate in the kitchen, my mother was the seasoned pro, but she always cheered me on whenever I tried to tackle a dish myself.

"Don't get too excited. I'm just warming up some leftovers from Napoli's."

"Now I'm jealous that I'm not there," she said with a laugh.

"There's no reason you shouldn't be. There's plenty of

food, and just because you don't live here doesn't mean that you can't visit. I can make up four plates just as easily as I can do three. What do you say?"

"I think that's the best offer I've had in some time," Momma replied. "Keep everything warm for me, and I'll be right there."

"I'm really glad," I said, excited to see her again.

As I got four plates ready, I found myself smiling, and I didn't even care if it made sense to anyone else or not. I was happy.

Taking the card table outside, I said to the two men, "I thought we'd eat out here together."

"You don't have to do that," Terry replied. "I don't mind eating alone."

"You may not, but I do, and I've got a hunch that my boyfriend isn't all that excited about leaving you out here by yourself, either. Jake, I'll go get the chairs. Can you manage the plates, the glasses, and the silverware?"

"Not in one trip, but I can do it," he answered. "It turns out that my left hand is more useful than I was giving it credit for."

"Yes, I'm sure you'll be playing the violin again in no time," Terry said with a smile. "Can I help out, too?"

"You just keep watch," I said. "That's more than enough."

"That I can do," he replied as he scanned the park around us. I knew that it wasn't the easiest place in the world to defend, but I wasn't about to go anywhere else.

Back in the kitchen, Jake asked, "Suzanne, why are there four plates? Do I get two servings, since I'm recovering from my gunshot wound?"

"I can grab seconds for you if you're still hungry after the first round, but that plate's for Momma."

"That's great," he said. "I'm glad that you invited her."

"To be honest with you, I miss her," I admitted.

"Why wouldn't you?" he asked tenderly. "This new arrangement has got to be a big adjustment for both of you."

I kissed him lightly, careful not to joggle his bad arm. "Thank you."

"For what?"

"Understanding me," I said.

"No thanks are necessary, but they are still greatly appreciated. Do I get another thank you for helping set the table?" he asked as he leaned in for another kiss.

"You *are* feeling better, aren't you?" I asked after I gave him another quick peck.

"More and more every minute," he said as he took a deep breath in. "That smells fantastic."

I pulled out the trays and put them on the stovetop. "You can't go wrong with Napoli's."

"The company's pretty good, too," he said.

"I agree. Now let's get busy. Momma's going to be here shortly."

"I'm on it," he said as he grabbed the plates carefully and made his way out with the first load.

"This has been lovely," Momma said as we finished eating on the porch together. Terry had insisted on sitting with his back to the door so he could keep an eye on the land around us, but he still managed to take part in the conversation, and eat a good amount of food as well.

"Mrs. Hart, it's been a real pleasure getting to know you," Terry said.

"As I told you before, it's Dorothea," she said, "or Dot, if you prefer."

"I'd prefer to stick with Mrs. Hart, but I can probably manage Dorothea." He gestured to the cottage. "This place is really something."

"Thank you," she said automatically. "It's been in the family for generations, and more to come, hopefully."

"Well, I don't plan on moving anytime soon," I said.

"Nothing would delight me more if you stayed here forever," Momma said as her cellphone rang. "Would you all please excuse me?"

We all nodded, and Momma stepped away from the table as she took her call.

Terry remarked, "That lady's the real deal, isn't she?"

"What do you mean?" I asked.

"The woman is so confident in her own skin that she's not afraid to say exactly what's on her mind." He must have thought about how that sounded, because the state police inspector quickly added, "Just in case you weren't sure, that was a compliment. I haven't met many folks like her in my life."

"And you most likely won't," Jake said. "She's one of a kind."

"I guess," I said. "To me, she's always just been my mother."

Jake smiled at me. "Kids are the hardest people in the world to impress, aren't they?"

"Aren't they what?" Momma asked as she rejoined us.

"These two nice gentlemen were just complimenting you," I said with a smile.

"I must say, I'm sorry that I missed that," Momma answered in turn. "That was Phillip. He stopped by my place and wondered where I was."

"You can invite him over, too," I said. "There's plenty of food left."

"I already did, but he just had a second to spare. He did have a message for you, though, Jake."

That clearly caught my boyfriend's attention. "What did he have to say?"

"As much as it displeases me to pass this on, Phillip believed that it was imperative that I share it with you. He said that Heather told him that it was important to tell you that she's already taken care of you and Suzanne. You just don't know it."

"The woman is clearly deranged," Terry said.

"There's little doubt about that," Momma answered.

"Should we be worried?" I asked Jake.

"No, she's not going to escape again, at least not anytime

soon. Suzanne, you can safely put her out of your mind."

"There's nothing that I'd like better," I said. I noticed that Momma was still standing beside us. "Have a seat."

"I'd like to, but I'm afraid that I have pressing business elsewhere. This was quite nice, though."

Both men stood, and Terry offered my mother his hand. "It was a pleasure, Dorothea."

"For me as well," she said, and then she kissed Jake's cheek lightly. "You get better soon, young man, do you hear me?"

"I'll do my best," he said.

After Momma was gone, the party just kind of broke up.

Jake started to help me clear the table, but I suggested, "You've done enough for now. Why don't you sit with Terry and I'll take care of this?"

"I hate to make you do all of the work," he said, but his smile told me that he didn't hate it that much.

"Don't worry. I'm saving up every favor you owe me."

"Wow, this is going to cost you a trip to Paris before it's all over," Terry said, teasing his friend good-naturedly.

"You know what? Paris sounds just fine to me, if Suzanne can drag herself away from the donut shop that long," Jake said seriously.

"Hey, I'm taking a month off to look after you, remember?"

Jake smiled at that. "I'm not sure that you'll even be able to last a week on the sidelines, let alone an entire month. That place is too much a part of you for you to ever leave it behind."

"You never know. I just might surprise you," I said.

"Suzanne, truth be told, there's nothing that I'd like more. Tell you what. Once I'm fully healed and cleared for duty, let's both take a week off and go on that trip. There's something about being shot that puts things in perspective in a hurry."

"It's a date," I said with a smile of my own. I just hoped that I could follow through. I was definitely feeling the tug of the donut shop being open without me being there, but did that mean that I could never leave it? I hoped not. When I'd first bought the place with my divorce settlement from Max, I hadn't imagined that it would rule my life, but if I was being honest with myself, that's exactly what it had done.

Maybe, with my boyfriend's help, I could break that particular spell.

After all, I always had wanted to see Paris, and I couldn't think of a better person to see it with than Jake.

Chapter 17

I watched her walking down the road toward her place, all alone. At one point she was so close to me that I could have easily reached out and grabbed her, but I wasn't quite ready to do that just yet. I had to make them both sweat a little before I moved on them. It was easy enough taking her picture with my phone, though. I'd find a way to use it soon to start the panic.

I wanted them both good and scared before I finished this.

Morton was going to get his revenge, even if it was going to be from beyond the grave.

Chapter 18

Thankfully, the rest of the day was fairly quiet, and by eight PM, I caught myself yawning. Despite my new schedule, my sleep patterns hadn't adapted to my new bedtime yet. At least Jake was tired, too.

"You're killing me with those yawns of yours," he said with a smile after a particularly spectacular one on my part. "I can't seem to stop myself from yawning, too."

"I'll try to quit, but old habits die hard," I said.

"Hey, we can call it a night right now if you'd like. I'm sure that I'll be able to get to sleep without trying too hard."

"Let's at least see if we can stay up until nine," I answered. "What do you think?"

"I'm game if you are," he said.

As it turned out, neither one of us had any trouble staying awake an hour later, but it had nothing at all to do with our sleep patterns.

"Chief, what are you doing here? Your shift doesn't start for hours yet, and Terry, you should be back at your hotel room by now," I said as I answered the door. I was surprised to find the state police inspector there with the police chief, since George had been on duty for just a few hours.

"I hate to do this, but you both need to come with me right now," the chief said grimly.

"Has something happened?" Jake asked as he grabbed his jacket.

"Is it Momma? Has she been hurt? Please tell me that she's all right." I had a sudden fear that Rusk had gone after someone I loved so much, however irrational that might be. I couldn't stand the thought that someone might have hurt her because of Jake or me.

"Don't worry. Your mother is fine," the chief said.

"Thank goodness for that," I replied.

"If no one's hurt, then what is it?" Jake asked Terry.

"I think that it's going to be better if you see it for yourself," Terry said. "Bear with me, okay?"

Jake nodded, and I followed him out the door. "Hey, George," I said as I walked past the mayor. "Are you coming with us, too?"

"No, I'm hanging back to keep an eye on the cottage," he said. "No worries here."

"I appreciate that," I answered, and then I turned to the men and asked, "Should I drive Jake to wherever we're going?"

"No, I want you all to come with me in my squad car," Chief Martin said.

"It might be nice to at least know where we're going," Jake said.

"Nathan's Sport Shop," the chief replied.

I'd been in Nathan's a few times, though his wares weren't really my general area of interest. Nathan catered mostly to hunters and fishermen, selling all kinds of specialty equipment and other things that outdoorsmen preferred. I happened to know that because the same group also made up a part of my own clientele at the donut shop. After all, it wasn't unusual during any hunting season to find them stopping into Donut Hearts for a little snack on their way in or out of town.

"What's going on at Nathan's?" I asked.

"He had a break-in," Terry said.

"That poses more questions than it answers," Jake replied.

"You'll see soon enough," Terry said, and we drove the rest of the way in silence.

Thankfully, we got there a few minutes later. Everything looked perfectly normal to me from the outside. "Where's the broken glass, in back?" I asked as we pulled into the parking lot.

"No, he was slicker than that. The alarm was bypassed and the lock was picked. This guy was a real pro," Terry explained.

"How do you know it was a guy?" Jake asked.

"Go on in and see for yourself," Terry answered.

I followed the three men inside, looking around as I walked through the place. There were still no signs of a robbery to my eyes, at least not the ones I would have expected. I tended to think of burglars as leaving behind smashed glass and broken items, but this theft was on a whole different level. The only thing amiss that I could see was a gun case standing open.

And then I saw the large white-board where sales were announced. I used one myself at the donut shop, but mine had never been used for something like this.

In a fine, almost delicate hand, it said,

"You can hire an army to protect you, but it won't do you any good. I'm coming for you, Jake. I could have taken Suzanne today, but I wanted you to feel fear deep in your gut before I moved in on you. You're going to have to watch me kill her, and then I'm going to take care of you. Rusk."

The message was creepy enough, but the attached photograph was even worse. It showed me, in clear detail, walking on the road between the donut shop and my home. The worst part about it was that I was wearing the same clothes in the photograph that I had on at the moment.

"This was taken today," I said, feeling my blood chill a little as I said it.

"We figured as much when we saw it," the chief said gravely.

"What all did he take?" I asked as I looked at the open gun safe with new fear.

"A good hunting knife, a handgun, and just two bullets," Terry said. "He wanted to be sure that we got his message. He's a cocky little murderer, isn't he?"

With quiet determination in his voice, Jake said, "He's going to pay for this."

"Don't you worry about that. We'll get him," Terry said. "Announcing what he's going to do just makes me that much more intent on catching him, and soon." He tapped the photograph with the cap of a pen. "I knew that was a bad idea when you did it. It can't happen again, Suzanne."

"It won't," I said. The photo hit me harder than the threats. I'd been right after all. Someone *had* been watching me from the park. "What can we do about it?"

"There's something else I need to tell you. I called the chief," Terry said, and then pointed to Chief Martin. "I should say our boss."

"I thought that we were going to handle this," Jake said icily.

Terry looked uncomfortable with the statement. "I didn't have any choice, and you know it."

Jake just shrugged. "What did he say?"

"He feels as though what we've been doing up until now isn't working too well, and he's decided to send a team tomorrow to relieve your volunteer guards." The state police inspector turned to the local police chief and added, "No offense intended to any of you, but this is one bad man."

"None taken," Chief Martin said. "I don't have any problem knowing when I'm in over my head."

"What are we supposed to do in the meantime?" I asked Terry. "Just sit around and wait for the troops to show up?"

"I brought up that exact same point, but since our boss is out of town, he can't make this happen any sooner. We just have to redouble our vigilance until then. I strongly suggest that you vacate the cottage in the meantime. It's clear that Rusk knows that you're there."

I was about to agree to relocating when Jake surprised me. "Terry, we're not going anywhere. I stand by what I said before. If we run and hide now, we'll lose all hope of catching this guy forever. If anything, we need to do something to flush him out before our reinforcements arrive."

Terry grinned. "I was hoping that you felt that way. That's my thought exactly."

"Are you two seriously going to use us as bait to catch this lunatic?" I asked him. I couldn't stand to look at my picture, or the taunting message Rusk had left us.

"Not you, Suzanne; me," Jake said firmly.

I laughed, but there was no joy in it. "Jake, I'm not leaving you alone, and that's final. No matter what happens, I'm staying in the cottage if you are."

"It's not going to happen, Suzanne," he barked.

I decided not to snap back at him, since I knew that he was under a tremendous amount of stress. To my surprise, Terry spoke up. "I think she's right, Jake."

"Have you lost your mind?" my boyfriend asked his fellow inspector.

"Think about it. If Suzanne is gone, Rusk might just vanish and try again later when everyone isn't watching out for him. We've discussed this before, but you need to make a hard and fast decision right now. Do you really want to spend the rest of your life looking over your shoulder?"

"You know that I don't, but that doesn't mean that I'm willing to sacrifice Suzanne, either."

"Nobody's being sacrificed," I said. "I trust you all. I'll be safe."

"You'd better be," Chief Martin said. "If something happens to you, your mother will take care of me herself, and nobody will ever find the body."

The fact that nobody tried to contradict him didn't do much to ease the frown on Chief Martin's face.

"If we're going to do this," Jake finally said, "then we'd better have the perfect plan in place, and we have to do it tonight."

"We both know there's no such thing as a perfect plan," Terry said. "All we can do is try to cover all of our bases and hope that we're smarter than he is."

Jake just shrugged, but I wasn't quite so nonchalant about it all. "But we're still going to try to come up with something that keeps us safe and traps him, right?"

Jake must have sensed the worry in my voice. "Suzanne, we won't do a thing unless all of us are confident that it's going to work. Otherwise, we'll go underground until the good guys show up tomorrow. How does that sound to you?"

"Better," I admitted. "So, who's got the first idea?"

Terry looked around the shop at the local cops milling about. Had they been listening in to everything that we'd been discussing? And worst of all, could Rusk find a way to torture one of them to get that information out of them? "Is there anyplace we can go where we won't be disturbed?"

"I can clear everyone out here," Chief Martin said as he looked around the room.

"I've got an even better idea," I replied. "Let's go over to Donut Hearts. I can make us all some fresh coffee, and if we stay in the kitchen, no one's going to bother us. At least it's away from the cottage, and any other prying eyes that might be eavesdropping on us."

"Speaking of reinforcements," the police chief said, "I'm calling Officer Grant in to team up with the mayor right now. No one pulls a shift alone until this thing is resolved, and I'm not about to leave one of my people hanging in the wind."

"That's a good idea," Terry said. "You should absolutely do that. It will show Rusk that we're taking him seriously, and it might even help us spring our trap."

"Then let's all go to the donut shop," I added.

The chief made arrangements with Officer Grant to join George immediately on the way to the donut shop. I let everyone in before locking up behind us, and as soon as I got into the kitchen, I flipped on a few lights and hit the coffee pot switch as well. It was too bad there were no donuts there. And then I saw three boxes sitting on the counter. It was my policy to get rid of extra donuts at the end of every working day, but evidently Emma and her mother had other ideas for these. I flipped the lids and found a nice assortment, so I laid them out and grabbed four cups as well. For once, I was glad that Emma had gone against my regular protocol. Those donuts would come in handy as we planned how we were going to lure Rusk into a trap without risking our own lives in the process.

An hour later, we finally managed to come up with a working plan, something that we all thought just might succeed in trapping the killer. There was some risk involved, no one denied that, but it was the best that we could do given the circumstances, so we decided to move forward.

Now all we needed was some cooperation from a killer, and a small crack in his armor that we could exploit. Otherwise, Jake and I would be on edge for the rest of our lives, and I for one wasn't willing to live that way, especially if we could end it all within the next few hours.

Chapter 19

The hardware store had been ridiculously easy to break into. I could have taken a ton of weapons with me as I left, but in the end, I decided that simple was best. One handgun and one knife would be plenty to finish them. I didn't even take a handful of bullets with me, either. I chose two randomly and loaded them into the gun. After all, two was all I planned to use.

Let them make of that what they would.

This should scare them.

And if they were jumpy, they'd soon make a mistake, and that's when I would hit them with everything that I had.

Now I just had to wait for the right time to strike.

One thing I knew for sure was that it would be soon.

Very soon.

Chapter 20

"Are we all set on your end?" Jake asked the local policeman a little later when Chief Martin finally returned to the donut shop. It felt as though Jake and I had been there forever, though Terry and the chief had been in and out a few times once we'd finalized our plans.

"I'll have everyone in place in under an hour," Chief Martin said a little unhappily. "I've got to say again for the record, the one thing I don't like about the plan is that I'm not going to be involved in it."

"That's not true at all," Terry said. "You and a few of your best men are going to be standing by waiting for our call. We could need you as reinforcements after we've sprung the trap, but you've got to remember that if there are too many people at the house, Rusk is never going to believe our setup. We have to sell this the first time, because we're only getting one shot at it."

"I can see your point, but that doesn't mean that I have to be particularly happy about it," the chief said reluctantly. After a moment, he sighed softly, and then he added, "Well, if that's the way that it's going to be, then I'd better get started on my end."

As he got up to leave, I stopped him. "Thanks for doing this, Chief."

"I know that it's important," he said. "Don't mind me. I'm just getting grumpy in my old age. Suzanne, be careful, okay?"

"I promise."

"I know that your mother will appreciate that, and so do I."

"She's nervous about this, isn't she?" I asked. I'd briefed her about our plans over the phone earlier, and after some discussion back and forth, she'd finally seen that Jake and I really didn't have any choice. That didn't mean that she had to like the idea of setting a trap any more than Chief Martin did, though.

"She understands why it's important to do this right now, but of course she's going to worry until this is all over." The chief paused, patted my shoulder gently, and then he added, "I'll go fetch your Jeep and park it right out in front of the shop. The keys will be on the left front tire."

"Aren't you worried that someone might steal it?" I asked him with a smile.

"I've seen your Jeep. I'm not that worried," he answered with a small grin of his own.

After the police chief was gone, Terry shook Jake's hand. "Give me half an hour before you go back to the cottage, okay? I need a little time to get things set up on my end."

"We can do that," Jake said.

"Good luck."

"Right back at you."

After Terry left, it was down to just my boyfriend and me. "Jake, is this really going to work?" I asked him softly.

"I hope so. After all, it's our best shot at catching him anytime soon."

"He's a pretty crafty guy though, isn't he? What happens if Rusk sees this for what it is, just a ploy to expose him?"

"Suzanne, I won't lie to you; he's clever. I didn't even realize the man existed until after I was shot. I'm not exactly sure what all he's capable of doing."

"But we've planned for every contingency as far as you can see," I said.

"Are you getting cold feet about all of this?" he asked me, the concern clear on his face. "You know, it's not too late to back out of this."

"No, the logic of it is all sound. We need to catch him while we can, no matter what the risk is."

Jake touched my shoulder lightly. "Don't worry. I'll be with you the entire time. Everything is going to work out just fine."

"Of course it will," I said, though I wasn't entirely sure that I believed it.

The next thirty minutes felt like a lifetime as we waited for the allotted half hour to pass, but it was finally time to head back to the cottage. “Are you ready?” Jake asked me.

“As I’ll ever be. How about you?”

“Are you kidding? I can’t wait to get started,” he said with a grin.

“You really mean that, don’t you?”

“Suzanne, I *hate* just sitting around waiting for something to happen. The only way that we have any chance of controlling the situation is by being proactive, and not reactive.”

“Is that cop talk for doing something instead of waiting around for something to be done to you?” I asked him with a slight smile as we exited the donut shop and walked to my Jeep.

“It’s just common sense,” he said. In a lower voice, he added, “Help me in. Remember, we need to sell this. If Rusk is watching, he needs to believe that I’m completely helpless.”

“I’ve got it. I’ll play my part convincingly,” I said as I took his good arm and practically shoved him onto the passenger seat.

Once we were both buckled in, I drove us back to the cottage. It took less than a minute to get there, but I fought the urge to look around the entire time we were on the road. I had an eerie feeling that we were being watched, and not just by the good guys.

As I parked in front of my place, Jake took my hand and squeezed it gently. “Remember, make it a good show.”

“I’m going to be so good that I’ll probably win an Oscar,” I said, trying to summon a smile I didn’t feel.

“Wait right there for me,” I said loudly as I walked around to Jake’s side of the Jeep. “You need to be careful getting out.”

“Suzanne, I’m so exhausted I don’t think I can make it up those steps,” he said loudly. I thought he was overdoing it, and I softly said so when I reached him. “Tone it down a little, Jake.”

"Sorry," he whispered as I helped him out. Jake stumbled a little, but I caught him before he fell. As I steadied him, I wasn't sure if he'd been acting, or if he really had lost his balance for a moment.

George had to have been listening to our exchange from his position on the porch. He hadn't been clued in about this part of our plan, since we wanted his behavior to seem normal to Rusk if he was watching our little play. "Do you two need any help?"

We hadn't thought about enlisting anyone else at this stage, but it was brilliant as I considered it. "That would be great. I'm afraid that Jake's not doing too well tonight."

George hurried down the steps, with Officer Grant close on his heels. "Take it easy," the mayor said as he helped steady Jake. Once he was ready to walk again, Officer Grant flanked him, and the two men helped Jake up the steps and inside the cottage.

"Take it easy, my friend. We're almost there," George said with encouragement as Jake stumbled a little again going inside.

Once the four of us had the door shut behind us, Jake straightened back up and smiled at the mayor and Officer Grant. "Thanks, guys. You were both great."

"Wow, you got better in a hurry," Officer Grant said with a smile. "What was that all about?"

"We need to talk about that," Jake said. "We've come up with a plan to smoke Rusk out of the woods tonight. Would you two care to help?"

"You betcha," George said enthusiastically. I knew that he loved being mayor, but his time as a cop had been one of the highlights of his life, and he clearly missed it. "What can we do?"

He wasn't all that pleased when Jake explained his role, though. After he finished telling them the plan, Jake asked, "Do you understand what it is we want you to do?"

"Sure," George said reluctantly, "but we can do more than that."

"After Phase One is over, you need to be ready to step in if you're needed, just in case. That goes for both of you."

"Understood," Officer Grant said, and then he touched George's arm lightly. "Come on, Mr. Mayor. Let's see how well we can sell this."

"Just watch me," George said with a smile. "If this is my part, I'm going to make the most of it."

"Just don't overdo it," I said.

"No worries there," George answered. "Come on, Stephen, let's go back outside before anyone gets suspicious about how long we're staying in here."

The two men left, and Jake looked at his watch. "It shouldn't be long, now."

"Would you like a pill for the pain before we get started?" I asked him.

"No, I'd rather be a little uncomfortable and still have a clear head if it's all the same to you," Jake said, and I didn't blame him a bit. I had never been all that fond of taking medication myself.

Twelve minutes later, as if on cue, we heard the first siren.

It clearly wasn't a police car, though.

Something nearby was obviously on fire.

At least that's what we wanted Rusk to believe as our plan went into motion.

Chapter 21

The next thing I knew, there was a heavy pounding on the front door.

When I opened it, George said loudly, "There's a fire on the other side of town! We hate to abandon you like this, but Officer Grant and I need to go right now!" He was speaking a little too loud for my taste. Would Rusk believe it? This part was crucial to our plan.

"Go! Don't worry about us. We'll be fine."

"Thanks," George said as he winked at me. Turning to Officer Grant, he said, "Let's go. We're out of here!"

They both got into the patrol car parked in the driveway and sped off into the night, lights flashing and siren wailing. All that was left out in front of the cottage was my Jeep. I took a few steps out onto the porch and looked around. The funny thing was that I didn't even have to pretend to be frightened. I was shaking in my shoes, worrying about what might happen next.

If Rusk *was* watching, that should have been all of the invitation that he needed.

Now all we had to do was wait to see if our trap actually worked.

Chapter 22

"Did I lock the bedroom window upstairs?" I asked Jake. "I opened it this morning to let in some fresh air, and now I swear I can't remember if I locked it back."

"Take it easy. I'm sure that you've just got a case of the nerves. You checked it, and I'm sure that Terry made sure that it was locked, too."

"I know that you're probably right, but I have to go upstairs and see for myself," I said, feeling a compulsion to make sure that the cottage was as secure as we could make it. "It will just take a second."

"Suzanne, we really need to stay together."

"I understand that, Jake, but I *have* to do this." While a part of me knew that I was acting irrationally, I couldn't seem to help myself.

"Go then, but be quick about it, okay?" Jake asked.

"I will," I said, and before I headed upstairs, I kissed Jake quickly. "I'll be back in two shakes."

I hurried up the steps, and as I got to the top, I was already regretting my decision to leave his side. Jake had been right. I knew that window was locked, but I had to make doubly sure.

The odd thing was, my bedroom door was closed when I got to the second floor landing.

I *never* closed it unless I was sleeping or napping. Terry must have done it when he'd come back to the cottage half an hour before Jake and I had returned. I didn't know where the state police inspector was hiding, that was part of the plan, but just knowing that he was somewhere in the house made me feel safer.

When I opened the bedroom door, though, all of that went away.

"You must be Suzanne. I'm pleased to finally meet you in person. Do me a favor and get in here, would you? You should know that if you make the slightest sound, you're going to regret it for the rest of your very short life."

I'd seen the flyer with his sketch earlier, so I immediately recognized the man the second I saw him. Rusk was holding a bloodstained knife delicately in his hand as he stood near the doorway into my room.

Looking past him, I saw State Police Inspector Terry Hanlan trussed up and lying on my bed.

Terry had clearly been bleeding, and his eyes were closed when I looked at him. I couldn't tell if he was dead or alive, but there was nothing that I could do for him at the moment.

I instantly knew what I had to do.

I had to warn Jake, no matter what the consequences might be. Nothing that this lunatic could threaten me with would be worse than what would happen to the love of my life if Rusk had his way.

"Jake! He's up here!" I shouted as I tried to slam the door in the killer's face. Rusk was too quick for me, though. He made a grab for my arm with his free arm, and I couldn't get away.

"I told you to shut up," he hissed.

"Terry is hurt!" I shouted in response.

I saw the knife go up in the air, and I had the worst feeling in that split second than I'd ever had in my life. I knew that I was about to die, and there was nothing that I could do about it. As the stained blade moved closer and closer to my chest, I struggled to move, to fight back, to at least make this man suffer for what he was about to do to me.

All thoughts of running away were now gone.

If I was about to die, I was going to go down fighting.

As the knife neared my chest, I let my legs go out from under me, straining Rusk's grip on me. He tried to adjust the trajectory of the knife, but he wasn't quick enough.

Now I had less than a second to press home my advantage.

With everything I had in me, I sprung into his stomach, using my head as a battering ram, exploiting my legs for every bit of power that they could generate.

I could feel some of his ribs breaking on impact, and there was a satisfying huff of air shooting out of his mouth as I made contact.

Most important of all, though, was the fact that he automatically eased his grip on me.

This was my chance.

Jerking my arm away, I was free.

And I was done fighting. Now it was time for flight.

Running for the stairs, I was nearly at the top step when I felt my feet go out from under me.

Rusk had somehow managed to grab my leg before I could make my escape.

I kicked out with my free leg, but it was no use. His grip was like a steel band around my ankle.

I wasn't getting away this time.

Chapter 23

"I'm going to kill you slowly and painfully for what you just did," Rusk whispered in a raspy voice, and I knew that he meant every word of it.

"Drop the knife," Jake said as his head appeared in the stairway. His left hand was holding his handgun, and I could see it shaking in his unsteady grasp.

I just prayed that Rusk wouldn't notice it.

But he did.

"Glad you could join us," Rusk said almost jovially. "Really, Inspector? Do you honestly feel like risking a shot in your condition? We all know that you're right-handed," he told Jake, almost laughing as he said it. "Even at this range, you're just as likely to shoot Suzanne as you are to hit me."

"Shoot him anyway!" I screamed.

"I told you to shut up," he snarled.

"That's it. You're out of warnings," Jake said as he pulled the trigger.

Unfortunately, the shot missed.

I held my breath, wondering if it was my last one, when I saw some motion coming from my bedroom. Terry, wounded though he was, had somehow managed to roll onto the floor. Using his trussed legs banded together as a weapon, he kicked out at Rusk, sending the knife clattering to the floor.

Rusk still had the handgun that he'd stolen from the store, though.

"I don't need that anymore anyway. There's no reason to be quiet now, since all of your friends are out fighting the fire," he said as he reached into his pocket for his handgun.

Jake fired again, and this time, he hit home. Rusk took the bullet in his right shoulder, and there was no way that he could retrieve his handgun now. Without hesitation, the killer turned and leapt for the window he'd come in through, not bothering to even open it as he dove through the glass. The man had some kind of monstrous strength to take a bullet like that and keep fighting.

"He's getting away!" I screamed as I reached out for Terry's head to comfort him. "Somebody stop him!" I yelled out into the night.

And then I heard one final shot.

Chapter 24

Evidently Rusk was down for the count, but all I could think about was this brave police inspector who'd put his life on the line for me and my boyfriend.

"Jake, are you okay?" I shouted out as I grabbed my cellphone with one hand while I cradled Terry's head in my lap.

"I'm fine. How about you?"

"I'm just a little shaken up. I might have a bruise or two tomorrow, but Terry's really hurt." I knelt forward and said softly into his ear, "Hang in there."

"It's all good. Don't worry about me. I'm not going anywhere," he said in a whisper.

"911," the dispatcher said.

"I need at least two ambulances at my place. This is Suzanne Hart."

"Do you need police backup, as well?" she asked.

"No, I think we've got that covered," I replied. "Tell them to hurry."

As the EMTs were carrying Terry down the stairs, I asked them, "How bad is it?"

"He's lost some blood, but it looks as though we got him in time," one of them replied.

"How about the guy outside?" Jake asked.

"The police chief shot him in the leg, but the vic's been shot at least twice as far as we could see. Chief Martin is still out there holding a gun on the guy, though. As a matter of fact, he insisted that we come up here and take care of this guy before we touched the one lying out on the grass, and from the way that he was waving that gun around, we weren't about to argue with him."

"He's a good man to have watching your back," Jake said.

As the stretcher neared Jake, Terry leaned over and asked him, "Are you okay?"

"Never better. How about you?" Jake asked with a grin. "Thanks, by the way."

"Are you kidding? We both should be thanking Suzanne. She's the one who distracted him long enough for me to kick him in the back."

"Hey, I shot the guy, remember?" Jake asked playfully. "Doesn't that count for something?"

"Not really," Terry answered with a grin. That's when I had a hunch that he was going to be okay.

Once Rusk was taken away, handcuffed to his stretcher with Officer Grant riding along beside him, Chief Martin joined Jake and me inside the cottage.

"I'm glad that you were there watching our backs," Jake told him.

"I can't believe that I shot him in the leg," the chief said. With a slight grin, he added, "I was actually aiming for his chest."

"Let's just keep that our little secret," Jake said.

"I don't care where you shot him. You're a hero either way in my book," I told him as I kissed his cheek.

"It was nothing. I was just doing my job," the chief said as he blushed a little. "Hang tight. Your mother is on her way."

"I figured that she would be," I said.

"She wanted me to tell you that you're welcome to stay with her tonight, given what's happened," the chief said.

"I appreciate the offer, but I'm not going anywhere," I said as I turned to Jake. "How about you?"

"I'm game staying here if you are. Besides, it should be safe enough now. As far as we know, there's no one out there who still wants to kill us now."

The next afternoon, Chief Martin came back to the cottage, but he wasn't alone, nor was he in uniform. He looked rather dashing in his suit, and Momma was absolutely lovely in a pale pink dress.

"Where are you two off to dressed up like that?" I asked

them as they walked into the living room.

"Actually, we were thinking about getting married in the park," Momma said.

"I think it's a fine idea," I replied, still not getting it. "But I was talking about right now."

"So were we," the chief said with the broadest smile I'd ever seen on his face.

"I'm confused," I said. "I thought you were going to wait until Jake was completely healed."

"We were," Momma admitted, "but after what happened last night, we decided that life was too short to wait. Do you mind?"

"Not a bit," I said. "I'm happy for both of you."

"Well, the judge is on his way, so you'd both better get dressed. The ceremony starts as soon as he shows up."

"Wow, you really are in a hurry," I said. "Give us ten minutes at least, okay?"

"I'll probably need a little more than that," Jake said.

"That's a first," I answered with a grin.

"What's that?"

"The man is going to take longer to get ready than the woman."

"I don't think that's even close to being a first today among the four of us," Momma said as she looked at the chief.

"What can I say? I couldn't get my hair to behave, and I wanted to look good for you," the chief protested, and then we all laughed together.

It turned out to be a beautiful day for a wedding, and despite any misgivings that I'd had once upon a time about these two people as a couple, I found myself crying during the ceremony. When the chief kissed Momma and they turned to us as husband and wife, I cheered right along with Jake.

"Congratulations," I said to the happy couple. "I'd offer you something to eat, but I'm afraid that all I have are leftovers."

"I've seen that fridge," Chief Martin said with a smile. "It would be crazy to say no to what's inside it." Almost as an afterthought, he turned to my mother and asked, "Is that okay with you, Dorothea?"

"I think that it's a lovely idea," she said, smiling at her new groom.

"I couldn't be happier," the chief said. It didn't matter that he'd just married my mother. He was still the chief in my mind. What exactly was I supposed to call him now? Even in my own thoughts I couldn't bear to call him Phillip quite yet. Dad was out of the question. He was my mother's husband, but I'd had a wonderful father who I'd loved with all of my heart. The chief and I had forged an odd friendship since he'd started dating my mother, but I'd never changed the way I addressed him. There was only one real way that I could resolve it, and this was the perfect time to do it.

"So, what should I call you now?" I asked him.

"I'd be honored if you'd just call me Phillip," he said.

"Then Phillip it is," I said, and I kissed his cheek. "Now, let's go eat, Phillip."

As we walked back to the house, Jake asked me, "Do you need any help in the kitchen?"

"How much help do you think you'll be with that busted wing of yours?" I asked him with a smile.

"Not much, but to tell you the truth, I just wanted to give the happy couple a little time alone," Jake admitted.

"Then yes, of course I need some help," I said.

Jake and I were in the kitchen and the newlyweds were out in the living room having a few quiet moments together. Jake was restless, puttering around as I worked on preparing our meal. It wasn't as though I didn't have enough selections still to choose from. We'd done our best to eat our way through the offerings from our friends, but we were still steadily losing ground, since more food kept coming in faster than we could consume it.

"Do we have any candy?" Jake asked me as he looked around the kitchen.

"There's pie, cake, and four other kinds of desserts in the fridge," I said absently as I put two large trays of food into the oven.

"No, I don't want to ruin my appetite. I just want something small. Hey, this is perfect," he said as he reached for a caramel.

As I heard him unwrapping the candy, something clicked in my mind, and before another moment passed, I knocked it from his hands.

"Hey, I was just going to have one," he protested as he bent to pick it up.

I held his good arm so that he couldn't do it, though. "Don't touch it. I think it's been poisoned."

Jake shook his head. "Just because Heather was eating them doesn't mean that they're all tainted," he said reasonably.

"Jake, remember what she said when she was arrested? I asked her what she was going to do to me, and she said that she'd already done it. That candy has been poisoned; I'm sure of it."

"When would she have had the opportunity to do it?" Jake asked, though I noticed that he'd lost all interest in the candy dish as a potential treat.

"Someone broke into the cottage before we found out about Rusk, remember? I've just been assuming that he did it, but what if it was Heather, instead? We know that she didn't take anything, but I'm willing to bet that she left something behind. Only she must have gotten frustrated when no one died immediately, so she was going to try to break in again and leave more tainted candy behind."

At that moment, the police chief rushed into the kitchen, and his face went ashen when he saw the candy on the floor. "Nobody ate any of that, did they?"

"No," I said. "Why?"

"On a hunch, I sent the candy we found where Heather was hiding to the lab. There was enough poison in each piece to kill whoever ate it. I just got the call."

"I'm willing to bet that a piece or two in here is poisoned as well," I said as I gingerly offered him the bowl.

The chief took out a baggy, and then he grabbed a paper towel and carefully collected the candy and its wrapper still on the floor after he took the bowl from me. "That was too close."

"Closer than you might think. Chief, I would have been dead if it hadn't been for Suzanne," Jake said, his voice shaking a little as he said it.

"I got lucky. That's all," I said as I started to shake a little after it was all over.

"Luck didn't have anything to do with it, and we both know it. Thank you, Suzanne," Jake said solemnly.

"You're welcome," I told him.

"Is everyone all right in here?" Momma asked as she joined us in the kitchen. "Phillip, you rushed out of the living room as though you'd seen a ghost."

"We're all fine," I said. "Momma, are you sure you wouldn't rather go someplace nicer for your wedding reception?" I asked her.

"Where could we possibly go that has more ambience than our kitchen?" she asked me.

"You're right, on both counts," I said as I hugged her again.

"I'm confused. Both counts?" Momma asked me.

"This place has all of the atmosphere anyone could ever need, and it will always be how you just described it. This is our kitchen, even if you aren't living here anymore. You know that, don't you?"

"Of course I do. I love you, daughter of mine."

"I love you, too, Momma," I answered.

And then, as if on cue, the oven timer went off.

"Is anybody hungry?" I asked the three of them.

Both men nodded.

"I'd stay out of our way if I were you," Jake said. "We're both starving."

"Then let's see if we can do something about that and get

everyone fed with this bounty."

As we ate, it felt so good to have my world back, even though it had changed forever less than an hour ago. Momma was a married woman again for the first time in a long time, and she was living somewhere else to boot, even though it was still in April Springs.

I wondered how our lives would change now that she and Phillip were married. After Jake recovered and went back to work, I'd be on my own in the cottage, truly alone for the first time in my life.

To my surprise, I found that I was looking forward to it. I'd gone from being Momma's daughter to Max's wife and then back to Momma's daughter again without ever experiencing what it was like to live by myself.

Not that I'd ever truly be alone.

After all, when Jake finished recovering from his bullet wound, he would be back in April Springs every time he got the chance whenever his job allowed it, and Momma was just a three-minute drive away. It didn't hurt that my best friend, Grace, was just a few steps down the road as well.

Still, for what it was worth, I'd have my own space, a place to call mine.

I loved every last person in my life, but it might be nice to finally be on my own.

RECIPES

TWIST ON AN OLD STANDBY

In the course of this series so far, I've included well over a hundred recipes for more donuts than any one person should ever eat. It occurs to me that it might not be a bad idea to go back every now and then and try different takes on basic ideas. These donuts are basic, but there's nothing mundane about the way they taste! Give them a try. I think you might just like them!

INGREDIENTS

Dry
2 packets rapid rise yeast (about half an ounce)
1/2 teaspoon salt
1/8 teaspoon nutmeg (fresh is best, but store-bought is good, too)
4-5 cups flour (cake flour can be substituted)

Wet
1 and 1/4 cups half and half (whole milk, 2 percent, or even 1 percent can be substituted)
1/2 cup granulated white sugar
1/3 cup water, warm
3/4 cup unsalted butter, melted
2 eggs, beaten

Glaze
4 tablespoons unsalted butter, melted
2 teaspoons vanilla extract
1/2 vanilla bean, scraped (optional for richer flavor, but a bit pricey)
1 and 1/2 cups confectioner's sugar
3-4 Tablespoons hot water, or as needed

Oil for Frying
Canola or Peanut Oil, about 1 quart

INSTRUCTIONS

In a small bowl, add the warm water and then sprinkle the yeast packets in. I like to use a wooden spoon for this step to give the yeast every chance. In three to five minutes, the yeast should be incorporated and there should be some foam on the top. After the yeast has dissolved, take a larger bowl and mix the yeast, salt, nutmeg, half and half, sugar, melted butter, and eggs together with a wooden spoon. After that is blended thoroughly, add 2 cups of flour and beat on low speed with a hand mixer until smooth. Next, add more flour, half a cup at a time, until the mixture pulls away from the sides of the bowl. On a floured surface, knead the dough by hand until it is smooth. Check the dough by touching it in the center with your finger. It should feel somewhat elastic at this point. Next, roll the dough out until it's about 1/2 inch thick, and then cut the donuts out with a donut cutter. If you don't have one available, try using two different sized glasses. This will do in a pinch. After all, this part of the operation isn't that precise. Cover the donuts loosely with a light cloth in a warm place for about an hour to give them a chance to raise. After forty minutes, bring your oil to 350 degrees F. As the oil is heating, melt the butter in a saucepan, then add the sugar, vanilla, and vanilla bean caviar. Mix thoroughly, thinning with hot water as needed.

When the oil reaches the proper temperature, fry the donuts in shifts, taking care not to overcrowd your frying pan. Turn the donuts as they rise to the surface and fry another few minutes. Total time could vary, but should take approximately 4-7 minutes total. Remove the donuts from the oil and place on a wire cooling rack. Dip your donuts into the glaze while they're still hot, and then enjoy!

Yields 6-8 donuts.

DIPPING DONUT STICKS

These are a favorite of ours in cold weather. While the basic recipe can be used for several different shapes and styles of fried donuts, we like ours as long and narrow rectangles, perfect for those who prefer their donuts dipped in coffee, hot chocolate, or anything else yummy. An added bonus is that you don't need special cutters for this donut, or be forced to improvise if you need to like the earlier recipe above. My favorite size for these are created by making cuts about an inch apart and four to five inches long.

INGREDIENTS

2 packets rapid rise yeast (about half an ounce)
1/3 cup water, warm
2 eggs, beaten
1 cup evaporated milk
1/2 cup unsalted butter, melted
1/2 cup granulated white sugar
1/2 teaspoon nutmeg (fresh is best, but store-bought is good, too)
1/2 teaspoon cinnamon
1/2 teaspoon salt
4-5 cups flour (cake flour can be substituted)

Simple Glaze
1 teaspoon vanilla extract
1 cup confectioner's sugar
1-2 tablespoons hot water, as needed

Oil for Frying
Canola or Peanut Oil, about 1 quart

INSTRUCTIONS

In a large bowl, add the warm water and then sprinkle the yeast packets in. Stir until somewhat incorporated. In four to five minutes, the yeast should be dissolved and there should be some foam on the top. It's important to use yeast before its expiration date, so if you're not getting any foam, check the date, and also the temperature of your water. After the yeast has dissolved, mix into the yeast blend the beaten eggs, evaporated milk, melted butter, white sugar, nutmeg, cinnamon, and salt. Once that's mixed in, add two cups of flour and mix thoroughly. At that point, you'll be adding a cup of flour at a time until you get a smooth and consistent ball of dough. Remove it from the bowl and turn it out onto a well-floured surface. Knead the dough for about five minutes. It should be smooth and elastic at this point. Cover the bowl with a towel and let it rest 15 minutes in a warm place that's not drafty. I like to use my oven, turned off, but with the light on. I find it emits enough heat to do the job properly.

Next, roll the dough out onto the floured surface until it's between 1/2 and 1/4 inch thick. Using your knife or a pizza wheel cutter, cut the dough into one-inch strips, then cut the strips to be 4 to 5 inches long. I've found that this size fries best in my particular fryer. Spray a cookie sheet with cooking spray, and then lay out your strips out so that they're not touching. This may take more than one cookie sheet. Put them back in the unlit oven and let them raise for another hour. They should come close to doubling in size by then. Heat your oil, and once it hits 350 degrees, fry these two or three at a time, taking care not to overcrowd your pot. After about three minutes, flip one over and check for a golden brown color. Let them go another three minutes, remove, and drain on a wire rack. While the next batch is in the pot, drizzle or dunk your sticks in the glaze and set aside to cool completely.

Yields 8-12 sticks.

MY VERSION OF CRONUTS

I get so excited when the world sits up and takes notice of donuts. The latest craze is a new invention called the cronut, a delightful cross between a donut and a croissant. While I'm not about to try to duplicate the donut chefs who originally created this confection, I've been able to come up with something that I think is delicious. This one's quite a bit more work than my usual offerings, so be warned, make sure you have a lot of free time the day you try these, because it's a much longer process than I usually prefer, but I thought that this would be fun to at least try.

INGREDIENTS

1 packet rapid rise yeast (about a quarter of an ounce)
1/4 cup water, warm
2 eggs, beaten
1/2 cup buttermilk (whole, 2%, or 1% will do fine as a substitute)
9 tablespoons unsalted butter, melted, divided into three portions of 3 tablespoons each
3 tablespoons granulated white sugar
1 teaspoon vanilla extract
1/2 teaspoon salt
1/2 teaspoon nutmeg (fresh is best, but store-bought is good, too)
1/2 teaspoon cinnamon

3-4 cups flour (cake flour can be substituted)

Cronut Glaze
1 cup confectioner's sugar
1/2 teaspoon vanilla extract

1-2 tablespoons buttermilk, as needed (whole, 2%, or 1% will do fine as a substitute)

Oil for Frying
Canola or Peanut Oil, about 1 quart

INSTRUCTIONS

I like to use my stand mixer for this recipe, but feel free to use a hand mixer or even a wooden spoon to incorporate all of the ingredients. In the mixer's bowl, add the warm water and then sprinkle the yeast packets in. Stir until somewhat incorporated. In four to five minutes, the yeast should be dissolved and there should be some foam on the top. After the yeast has dissolved, mix into the yeast blend the beaten eggs, buttermilk, 3 tablespoons of the melted butter, white sugar, vanilla extract, salt, nutmeg, and cinnamon. Mix on low for about one minute, or until it's all incorporated. Once that's mixed in, add in one and a half cups of flour and mix thoroughly, still with the whisk attachment. At that point, you'll be adding a cup of flour at a time until you get a smooth and consistent ball of dough. Change over to a dough hook before you add more flour. Once the ball has formed and pulls away from the side of the bowl, turn it out onto a floured space and knead for about one minute and shape it into a ball. Wrap the ball in plastic wrap and put it in the refrigerator for 25 to 30 minutes. After that time, take the dough out of the fridge, unwrap it, and dust it with flour. Next, roll the dough out onto the floured surface until it's somewhere between 1/2 and 1/4 inch thick. Spread 3 tablespoons of the remaining melted butter on the center portion of the dough, fold a third of the dough over, spread 3 more tablespoons over the folded part, and then complete the fold with the last third of the dough. Spray a cookie sheet with cooking spray, and then place your dough on the sheet. Cover it lightly with plastic wrap and return it to the refrigerator for another half hour. After the half hour is up, remove the sheet from the fridge and put the dough on a floured surface. Gently pat it out until it forms a sheet about 8 inches by twelve. It should be anywhere between 1/2 and 1/4 inch thick at this point. Fold the dough into thirds again, and then place on the resprayed cookie sheet, covering with plastic wrap again. Refrigerate for 2 and 1/2 to 3 hours. After that time has elapsed, take out the cookie sheet and transfer the dough to the lightly floured surface again. Roll out the dough again until it's around 1/2 inch thick all the way around. Using your donut cutter, cut out donuts from the dough, place on a sprayed cookie sheet, and let rise for about an hour in your unheated oven with the light on for gentle warmth. Heat your oil, and once it hits 350 degrees, fry these two or three at a time, taking care not to overcrowd your pot flipping them after about two minutes on one side. These will puff up as they cook, so don't worry about it. Drain the cronuts on a wire rack, and then drizzle them lightly with the glaze recipe above.

Yields 10-14 cronuts.

CHOCOLATE SIN DELIGHTS

These donuts incorporate chocolate and cinnamon (the sin in the title), two of my favorite ingredients! The house smells amazing whenever I make these, and they're particularly good with chocolate icing straight from the container if you don't have the time or the ingredients for making a chocolate glaze yourself, an added decadence. Try them when you're feeling a little blue, and they're bound to lift your spirits!

INGREDIENTS

1 1/4 cups granulated white sugar
2 eggs, beaten
1/2 cup half and half (whole milk, 2 percent, or even 1 percent can be substituted)
2 squares grated chocolate, about 6 tablespoons
2 tablespoons unsalted butter, melted
2 teaspoons baking powder
1 tablespoon cinnamon
1 teaspoon nutmeg (fresh is best, but store-bought is good, too)
dash of salt
2-3 cups flour (cake flour can be substituted)

Oil for Frying
Canola or Peanut Oil, about 1 quart

INSTRUCTIONS

In a large bowl, beat together the sugar, eggs, milk, chocolate, and butter. In a separate bowl, sift together 2 cups of flour, baking powder, cinnamon, nutmeg, and salt. Gently stir the dry ingredients into the wet until thoroughly mixed. Continue to add flour until the dough is no longer sticky to the touch and can be rolled out. When it's ready, roll it out onto a floured surface until the dough is 1/2 to 1/4 inch thick, and then cut out your donuts using a cutter. Bring your oil to 350 degrees F in a large pot or skillet. When the oil reaches the proper temperature, fry the donuts in shifts, taking care not to overcrowd your frying pan. Turn the donuts as they rise to the surface and fry another few minutes. Total time could vary, but should take approximately 4-7 minutes total. Remove the donuts from the oil and place on a wire cooling rack. Dip your donuts into the glaze while they're still hot, and then enjoy!

Yields 6-8 donuts.

PILLSBURY® INSPIRED SWEET AND EASY TREATS

I like to include at least one easy recipe for donuts in each book, but sometimes that means repeating myself, something I try hard not to do. But let me tell you, after 13 books in the series featuring hundreds of recipes, sometimes the donutmaking is harder than writing the book! I've long been a fan of using premade doughs for quick treats, and Pillsbury® is my favorite brand. I'm not even getting paid for saying that! I stumbled upon this idea while doing some research for new donuts to bring you, and I found the idea both delightful and intriguing. Go ahead and give them a try sometime!

INGREDIENTS

1 can Pillsbury® crescent dinner roles
pudding flavor of your choice, about 4 ounces. Excellent choices include chocolate, banana, and vanilla
sauce of your choice, caramel, chocolate, strawberry, etc

Oil for Frying
Canola or Peanut Oil, about 1 quart

INSTRUCTIONS

Bring your oil to 350 degrees F in a large pot or skillet while you're preparing your filled donuts. Separate the crescent rolls into rectangles. Pair them up and pinch the edges to seal them so they don't come apart when they are frying. Once the rectangles are paired and sealed, fold them in half, sealing the edges again. You can fry them like this, or use your donut cutter if you prefer round shapes. When the oil reaches the proper temperature, fry the donuts in shifts, taking care not to overcrowd your frying pan. Turn the donuts as they rise to the surface and fry another few minutes. Total time could vary, but should take approximately 4-6 minutes total, or until golden brown on each side. Remove the donuts from the oil and place on a wire cooling rack. Once they're cooled, gently split the donuts open and spoon or pipe pudding filling onto the gap. Top them with any sweet sauces you prefer, or you can drizzle a glaze on top, and then enjoy!

Yields 2 quick donuts.

If you enjoy Jessica Beck Mysteries and you would like to be notified when the next book is being released, please send your email address to newreleases@jessicabeckmysteries.net. Your email address will not be shared, sold, bartered, traded, broadcast, or disclosed in any way. There will be no spam from us, just a friendly reminder when the latest book is being released.

Also, be sure to visit our website at jessicabeckmysteries.net for valuable information about Jessica's books.

Made in the USA
San Bernardino, CA
22 April 2018